CROSS OF IRON, HEART OF GOLD

BY: JACQUELYN BISHOP

Table of Contents

DEDICATION

For my father, Harold Ashley, and my father-in-law, Ted Bishop
With love and gratitude for the values you lived by—
honor, kindness, and strength.

PROLOGUE

1916 Germany

A military hospital not far from the Western Front

The Great War began with a spark and spread like wildfire across Europe, consuming everything in its path. What was meant to be a brief conflict of pride and alliances became a grinding storm of steel and sorrow — where nations bled, and the world learned the true cost of progress.

By 1916, the thunder of artillery had become the heartbeat of the continent. The air itself seemed to tremble with the roar of distant guns, and the earth had turned to mud under the endless rain of shells. Men lived and died in trenches carved from despair, while behind the lines, hospitals overflowed with the broken remains of youth and hope.
In the autumn of 1917, Germany was locked in a brutal war against the Allied Powers—Britain, France, and their allies—its soldiers entrenched along the Western Front, where every inch of mud was paid for in blood.

* * *

The night trembled with thunder that was not born of storms.

Outside the canvas walls of the field hospital, the earth itself seemed to convulse—each explosion sending a shudder through the ground, through the cots, through the bones of those who listened.

Inside, the air was thick with ether and fear. Lanterns swung on their hooks, casting frantic shadows across rows of bloodied stretchers. The stench of iodine fought a losing battle against the iron scent of blood.

Anna Müller didn't lift her head to see the shells anymore. She could tell their distance by sound—the long whine, the pause, the thud. The front was close. Too close.

But still she worked, her voice steady, her hands sure, the world narrowing to this small patch of trembling light in the middle of hell.

The next shell landed so close that the shockwave punched through the tent, snuffing out one of the lanterns and showering everyone in a rain of dust and debris. Someone screamed. A nurse stumbled, clutching her ear. Instruments clattered from a tray to the dirt floor.

"Keep working!" the doctor barked. His voice was hoarse from shouting over the endless thunder of guns.

Through the haze of smoke and falling dust, Anna caught the sound of boots pounding toward the entrance— heavy, uneven, dragging. The flap flew open again, letting in a blast of cold, acrid air thick with the smell of gunpowder.

"Make way!" cried one of the stretcher-bearers. "Critical—shrapnel wound, left leg—lost a lot of blood!"

"Shellfire at Hill 47," the other bearer panted. "We barely made it back."

The young man on the stretchers was streaked in mud and soot. His uniform was torn at the thigh, dark with blood. Beneath the grime she caught flashes of pale skin, the gleam of metal lodged deep in muscle. His eyes, a startling gray-blue, fluttered open for an instant.

Anna was already in motion. "Set him down here!" she ordered, her German accent clipped and steady, though her hands trembled slightly as she reached for the scissors.

The stretcher was set down with a thump, and then the men stumbled back out through the flap, back out into the madness outside.

For a heartbeat, the chaos receded as she looked upon the man they had brought in. His muddy face was set in pain. She quickly cut through the blood-soaked trouser leg with practiced precision, revealing the wound: a jagged gash, glistening red and black, split open by a dirty shard of metal. Her stomach twisted, but her hands did not falter. She ran a gentle hand over his knee, felt the tremor that went all the way up his thigh. "You're safe," she said, as much to steady her own breath as his. "You're here."

His face was pale, his eyes closed, his lips moving. She leaned over him, bending low, catching the faintest whisper of a prayer over the cacophony of the ward. The soldier's eyes fluttered open for a moment, glazed with exhaustion and pain, but still holding a spark of defiance, of life not yet surrendered. His lips moved. "Herr Jesus," he whispered, not quite a prayer and not quite an oath.

"What's his name?" she called.

"Lukas Schneider," came the reply from a nurse consulting the field log. "Infantry. Pulled from the line near Arras."

"Lukas," Anna repeated softly, testing the name as she pressed her palm to his shoulder. "You're very brave. Stay with me."

He gave the faintest nod, his jaw tightening as she poured antiseptic over the wound. He gritted his teeth, but the pain forced a groan from deep in his chest.

"I know," she whispered. "I know it burns. Almost done."

"Hold on," she murmured, leaning close so he could see her face through the dim. "You're safe now. You're at the hospital. We will not let you go."

He tried to speak, but the sound that came out was a rasp of pain.

Anna gestured sharply. "Get me clean water, morphine, and a tourniquet—quickly!"

Outside, the guns continued their dreadful rhythm—deep booms, sharp cracks, a ceaseless roar like the breath of a monstrous beast. Occasionally the sky flickered pale blue through the seams of the tent, the ghost-light of distant explosions.

"Pulse weak," murmured the orderly beside her.

"Hold pressure," Anna said. Her fingers pressed hard against the wound, feeling the man's life slipping through her gloves. "Morphine, half dose. Quickly!"

A doctor moved past, his face streaked with sweat despite the cold. "We're running out of clean bandages," he snapped.

"We'll boil more," Anna replied. "We'll make do."

The surgeon came, took one look, and swore under his mask. "Wash. Debride. He'll keep the leg if the rot doesn't set in." His eyes flicked to Anna. "You hold him."

For a moment, the thunder of distant artillery seemed to fade as the wind howled outside the canvas walls of the field hospital.

Anna adjusted the oil lamp to better see her patient's leg. Lukas, though pale and drawn from blood loss, clenched his jaw and tried not to flinch as she inspected the wound.

Somewhere to their left, another soldier began to scream—a raw, animal sound that cut through even the booming of the guns. The tent's thin canvas walls could not keep it out. Neither could they keep out the whistling descent of incoming shells.

A sudden explosion sounded alarmingly close. The ground leapt. Bottles rattled. A lantern fell and shattered, sending flame licking up the side of the tent until a medic smothered it with a damp blanket.

"Are we hit?" someone shouted.

"No—just near," came the answer, though the reassurance rang hollow.

Anna barely heard them. She focused on the man before her, on the color fading from his lips. "Stay with me," she whispered, though he could not hear over the distant artillery. "Stay with me."

For a moment, the thunder of distant artillery seemed to fade, and there was only the fragile thread of his life, and her hands determined to hold it fast.

CHAPTER ONE:
Meeting in Ashes

She tied the tourniquet tight and glanced at the orderly. "Pressure here. Keep it steady. He'll lose the leg if we don't stop the bleeding."

The doctor hurried over, eyes flicking to the wound. "He's lucky it didn't take him clean through."

"Lucky," Anna murmured, though her gaze lingered on the shrapnel still embedded in the flesh. She surmised that he didn't feel so lucky.

"Help me hold him," the doctor said.

She did. They worked by lantern light, their shadows jerking across the tent walls as the tools gleamed wet in their hands. She braced Lukas's shoulders while the surgeon poured warm saline and carbolic. Lukas arched with a harsh, bitten sound. Sweat sprang from him; he tried to twist away, and Anna leaned closer until the brim of her white cap brushed his temple.

"Look at me," she murmured. "It will pass. I promise you."

The soldier's eyes fluttered open for a moment, glazed with exhaustion but still holding a spark of defiance, of life not yet surrendered.

Up close, she saw how young he was, not much older than herself—twenty, perhaps twenty-one. His jaw clenched. He kept his eyes on her while the surgeon worked, while the forceps slid into the torn flesh and came out glistening with a shard of metal. When the fragment finally came free, Lukas gasped—half scream, half breath—and then sagged back against the cot, sweat beading his brow.

He kept looking when the needle dipped and rose, neat stitches closing the brutal rent.

"Good," Anna breathed, her hand firm on his shoulder. "Good, Herr Schneider. Very good." Then she turned to the orderly."Bandages," she ordered. "Tight."

Lukas didn't faint, but when it was over, he lay panting.

She cleaned the blood from his skin as gently as she could, brushing aside a lock of damp hair from his forehead. He was pale beneath the grime, his lips trembling slightly.

"Water?" Anna asked.

He nodded. She brought the enamel mug to his lips and tilted it carefully. He drank; some ran from the corner of his mouth into the stubble on his chin. She dabbed it away with a clean cloth.

"Your name?" he asked, voice raw.

"Anna," she said, and then, because good manners survived where other things did not, "Fräulein Müller."

"Anna," he repeated, as if the syllables mattered. "Ich—danke schön."

"Rest now," she said, her tone soft. "The worst is finished for today. You're safe, do you hear me?"

His eyes opened again—clear, searching her face as though trying to fix it in memory.

"Danke," he whispered.

The word was faint, barely audible over the thunder outside, but she heard it.

She tucked the blanket to his hip, the clean dressing already pinking. The surgeon moved on to the next bed, leaving her to finishing dressing he wound.

Anna paused, her hand still resting on his chest, feeling the weak but steady thud of his heart. Beyond the canvas walls, the battle still howled. But inside this small tent, for one fleeting moment, there was only the rhythm of his breathing and the quiet determination that she would not let him die.

The ward quieted to its familiar chorus of discomfort and endurance. Somewhere, an orderly laughed too loudly at a joke that wasn't funny.

* * *

The fever came with the darkness.

The warmth of the small portable stove did little to chase the chill from the air that evening. The night had settled, stars cloaked by a thin veil of clouds.

And yet within the chamber where Lukas lay, there was no peace. His skin, pale and clammy, glistened with sweat despite the woollen blankets wrapped tightly around him. Anna had only just finished helping him change into clean clothes when she noticed the flush deepening on his cheeks—and the tremble in his hands.

"Lukas?" she whispered, brushing her fingers against his forehead. The heat startled her. "You're burning up."

Lukas turned his head slightly, a soft moan escaping his cracked lips. He didn't answer.

Anna immediately summoned an orderly, who came with haste. "Fetch water," Anna ordered. "And rags. He's taken a fever—and it's a bad one."

"What's happened?" he asked, moving toward the bed.

Anna looked up. "The fever came quickly. We must bring it down or it will turn worse by morning."

He glanced at Lukas, then at her. "Tell me everything you need."

The field hospital was heavy with the scent of carbolic and sweat, the canvas walls trapping both heat and dread. Lukas lay half-propped on a cot, his thigh swaddled in hastily changed dressings already seeping through. The shrapnel had been removed, but infection had taken root, burning through him with a cruel persistence.

By nightfall, Lukas's skin was on fire. The color had returned to his cheeks, but it was the wrong kind—flushed and feverish, the glow of a body at war with itself. The cot creaked beneath him as his limbs twitched, sweat darkening the linen sheets Anna had only just changed.

Anna hovered beside him, her eyes gritty with exhaustion, her cool hands smoothing the damp hair from his brow. His skin burned under her touch, fever-flushed and clammy. Every so often, he muttered words tangled with half-coherent fragments of prayer and battlefield cries. She hushed him gently, pressing a cloth cooled in the basin to his forehead.

The storm outside had quieted, leaving behind a heavy stillness broken only by the crackle of the brazier and the rasp of Lukas's ragged breaths.

She soaked another cloth in cool water and laid it across his forehead. "Easy, Lukas," she murmured. "You're safe now."

But he didn't hear her—not really. His head turned from side to side, his mouth forming words she couldn't catch. Fragments escaped—half-coherent, half-dreamed.

"Hold the line… Weber, down—get down!" His voice broke, hoarse and desperate. He tried to sit up, his muscles jerking against her hands. "Anna—where—?"

"I'm here," she whispered, pushing gently against his shoulders. "You're not there anymore. You're in the hospital. Listen to me, Lukas."

But his eyes stared past her, unfocused, glassy with fever. He flinched as though from an unseen explosion. "We're surrounded—God, the smoke—" He choked, gasping, his chest heaving as though drowning in the memory.

Anna gripped his shoulders tighter. "Lukas! Look at me."

For a heartbeat, his gaze met hers—and then his expression crumpled. "I couldn't save them," he rasped. "They were crying out in pain, and I—"

Her throat closed. "Stop. You did what you could. You came back."

He was shaking violently now, his breath ragged, his body fighting the heat burning through him. She fetched the basin again, wrung out the cloth, pressed it to his neck, his wrists. Her fingers brushed against the thudding pulse in his throat—it was racing far too fast.

"Stay with me," she whispered, again and again, as if the repetition alone could anchor him.

Outside, the night stretched long and merciless. The oil lamp sputtered low. She listened to his muttering fade into gasps, then silence, then a fresh wave of shivering. She changed his bandages, her hands steady despite the trembling inside her. Each time she pressed her palm to his skin, she could feel the fire under it.

When the fever spiked, he called her name again. "Anna… don't leave me."

She froze. "I'm not leaving," she said softly. "You hear me? I won't ever leave you."

He exhaled, the tension in his body easing for the briefest moment. The line of his brow softened, and he sank back into uneasy sleep.

All through the day and into the night, she tended him— changing compresses, urging water past his lips, whispering soft reassurances. The fever raged on, his body shuddering with chills that turned moments later into sweats. Candlelight flickered across her face, drawing shadows under her eyes, but she refused to leave him.

When the ward grew quiet, the other nurses catching moments of rest between waves of casualties, Anna stayed. She leaned close when his breathing grew ragged, her fingers closing around his as if willing her own strength into him.

"Hold on, Lukas," she whispered, her voice frayed but steady. "You are not alone. Not while I am here."

Anna sat through the hours that followed, her head bowed, her hand resting on his arm. She could smell the sharp tang of antiseptic, the faint sweetness of morphine, and beneath it—the living, human scent of him, fragile and real.

Once or twice, she thought she heard him murmur her name again, softer this time.

The sharp stench of carbolic acid still lingered as the afternoon sun slanted across the narrow windows of the makeshift hospital ward. Cots lined the tent walls, each occupied by soldiers caught in the bloody churn of the Western Front.

Anna had just finished changing the bandages on another patient when she caught sight of Lukas shifting restlessly. She rushed to his side.

"Lukas," she murmured, kneeling beside him.

His brow was slick with sweat. His breaths were shallow, fast. She brushed damp curls away from his forehead, her hand trembling slightly.

"It's burning," he whispered, his voice strained. "My leg… Anna, I—I can't feel my toes."

Her heart clenched. That was a bad sign.

Anna unwrapped the wound carefully. A sour smell rose with the steam from the infected tissue. The wound on his thigh, a jagged tear from shrapnel, had gone from angry red to a sickly purple along the edges.

She bit her lip to keep from showing her alarm.

She called for another nurse and had Lukas's cot moved closer to the stove for warmth. Then she washed her hands, tied on fresh gloves, and began preparing a poultice of iodine and sterile gauze.

"You need to be brave, Lukas," she said gently, trying to keep her voice steady. "The wound is angry, but I'll do everything I can. You hear me?"

His eyes met hers, glassy but searching. "Stay with me, please. Just stay."

"I will," she whispered, adjusting the morphine dose to ease his pain. "You're not alone."

Anna sat by Lukas's cot as he burned with fever. The faint candlelight flickered across his pale, sweat-soaked face. His fingers twitched, lips murmuring fragments of battle and names she didn't recognize. She gently dipped a cloth into cool water and pressed it to his brow.

"Hush now," she whispered, her voice tender. "You're safe here. I've got you."

When he cried out in his sleep, she took his hand, rubbing soothing circles into his palm. It was in those quiet, breathless hours of the night that her feelings grew—no longer just nurse and patient, but something deeper, unspoken.

The fever clung to Lukas like a wet sheet, drawing sweat from his brow even as he shivered beneath the blanket. His cheeks were flushed, his lips cracked. Anna sat at his side, dabbing his forehead with a damp cloth and whispering softly in hopes her voice might reach him through the haze.

The staff doctor entered with his medical bag, his expression grave as he glanced from Anna to the soldier writhing on the cot.

"Nurse Müller, thank you. Let me see the wound."

Anna stood but didn't move far, unwilling to leave Lukas completely.

The doctor peeled back the bandages, and Anna gasped despite herself.

The wound on Lukas's thigh was deep purple, red and swollen. Jagged pieces of shrapnel had torn through muscle, leaving blackened edges and signs of infection. The stench was unmistakable.

"It's necrotic," the doctor muttered. "If the infection reaches the bone—if it hasn't already—it will spread through the bloodstream."

He looked at Anna, grim. It did nothing to ease the growing worry in Anna's heart.

"The fever tells me we are already behind. If he doesn't respond to carbolic acid cleansing or cauterization, amputation may be the only option to save his life."

Anna's chest tightened. Lukas groaned, his head rolling to the side.

"He's fought so hard to get here," she whispered. "Is there truly no other way?"

The doctor didn't answer right away. He reached into his bag and began preparing tools, laying out clean gauze, scissors, and forceps.

"We will try to clean the wound and see if he responds to aggressive treatment. We'll watch the fever. If he worsens by morning…"

He let the silence speak for him.

Anna swallowed hard, gripping Lukas's hand as the doctor leaned over him.

* * *

At dawn, when the light began to seep through the canvas, his fever still had not broken. She lifted her tired gaze to the pale sky and prayed silently that this day would not be his last.

The hours crept by with the slow cruelty of a clock that refused to move. Each time Anna thought Lukas's breathing had steadied, a new shudder racked his frame, or a broken groan slipped past his lips. His hand, hot and trembling in hers, sometimes went slack, and she would jolt upright, terrified that his strength was gone.

"Stay with me," she whispered again and again, though she knew he could not truly hear her.

The fever painted his cheeks with a deep, unnatural flush, his body soaked with sweat. She replaced the compress on his brow for what felt like the hundredth time, dipping the cloth into cool water that was already warm by the time she wrung it out. Her own sleeves were damp, her hands raw from hours of tending, but she did not leave his side.

Around them, the ward was hushed except for the groans of other men and the low rustle of nurses moving softly between cots. The lantern flame wavered, throwing shifting shadows across Lukas's face, making him seem already half-ghost, caught between worlds.

Anna's heart clenched with every ragged breath. She bent close, so her forehead touched the back of his hand, the words of a prayer rising unbidden to her lips. *HaShem, please do not take him.* She meant it.

When at last the bell tolled midnight outside, Lukas stirred—his eyes flickering open for only a moment. She caught the faintest whisper, hoarse and almost soundless. Her name. Then he sank back into fevered dreams, leaving her shaken, uncertain if she had truly heard him or if exhaustion had played a trick.

Still, she clung to that fragile thread, sitting vigil in the flickering dark, willing him to live through just one more hour.

* * *

The night had seemed endless. Anna's eyes burned from lack of sleep, and every muscle in her back ached from leaning over his cot. Yet she dared not rest—not when his pulse fluttered beneath her fingers, not when each breath came with such effort it seemed the next might be his last.

The lantern had guttered low, its light a pale circle against the canvas wall, when she felt it: a shift. Subtle at first, almost imperceptible. Lukas's skin, which had burned like fire all night, grew damp with a different kind of sweat—cooler, as though the fever's grip were loosening.

She pressed the cloth once more to his brow, then drew it back quickly, her heart catching. It wasn't as hot as before. Still warm, yes, but no longer searing. Her breath trembled out, half a sob, half a prayer.

Outside, the first grey of dawn seeped through the seams of the tent, softening the darkness. The change of light seemed to mirror the change in him. His chest rose and fell in a steadier rhythm, the frantic flush of his cheeks fading just a shade.

Anna brushed damp hair from his forehead, her hand lingering there, afraid to hope too much. "Lukas," she whispered, voice thick with tears. "Stay with me. You're winning this fight."

His lashes fluttered, though his eyes did not open. A faint sound stirred in his throat—less a word than a sigh, but it was enough to make her shoulders sag in relief. She bowed her head over his hand, finally allowing herself to breathe, the first tendril of hope stealing back into her heart with the pale light of morning.

Lukas, half-conscious, heard her humming Hebrew prayers under her breath.

* * *

When dawn finally touched the horizon, pale and cold, Lukas's fever began to break. The sheen of sweat cooled on his skin. The heat had broken at last, leaving Lukas weak, his skin pale and damp, but his breathing steadier. Anna kept vigil beside him, washing his brow, adjusting his blankets, whispering words of comfort he only half-heard.

The lamp flickered out. In the dim, quiet light of morning, she kept her vigil—one hand still resting over his heart, feeling it beat steady and sure beneath her palm.

He had come back to her, and she would not let him slip away again.

* * *

The days that followed were quieter than the fevered night that had nearly stolen him away.

By the third morning, when the winter light spilled through the canvas of the hospital tent, he stirred more clearly. His hand shifted against the sheets, and his voice—hoarse but steady—murmured her name.

"Anna…"

Her heart leapt. She bent close, smoothing his hair back from his temple. "You're safe. You've come through the worst."

His eyes fluttered open, heavy with exhaustion, but there was recognition in them at last. He caught sight of her and managed a faint smile, one corner of his mouth tugging upward. "You never left me."

"I couldn't." Her voice broke on the words. "Not when you fought so hard."

The wound in his thigh was still angry and raw, but each day she cleaned it carefully, wrapped it with fresh bandages, and coaxed him to take broth or sips of water. Slowly, his strength returned. He no longer drifted endlessly in fevered dreams; now he could sit up a little, even joke weakly with her.

One evening, as she adjusted his pillow, Lukas reached out and caught her wrist—gently, but with a steadiness that hadn't been there before. "You've saved me twice over," he said. "From the battlefield—and from the fever."

23

Anna felt warmth bloom in her chest. Their bond, forged in pain and survival, was becoming something deeper, something neither the war nor the world outside could erase.

* * *

Dawn came quietly, like a truce that no one quite trusted. Lukas, half-conscious, heard Anna murmuring Hebrew prayers under her breath. The guns had fallen silent sometime before sunrise, leaving behind a strange, echoing stillness that felt heavier than the shelling itself. Smoke still drifted low over the fields beyond the tents, curling through the pale gray light.

Inside the medical ward, the night's chaos had ebbed to a weary hush. Men slept fitfully beneath coarse wool blankets. A few murmured in dreams; others did not move at all. The nurses worked in silence, eyes hollow from exhaustion, their aprons stiff with dried blood.

Anna moved slowly between the cots, her steps soundless on the dirt floor. She carried a basin of warm water, the steam faint against the chill morning air. Her hands ached, and her back felt as though it had aged twenty years in a single night. But there was still work to be done. Always more work.

She stopped at the third cot on the left.
Lukas.

He lay half-propped on his side, the bandages around his thigh clean but tight, his breath shallow yet steady. The lantern beside his bed had burned down to a stub, its wick curling in a pool of wax. She set it aside and dipped a cloth into the basin.

His eyes fluttered open as she touched the cloth to his forehead. They were gray-blue still, though rimmed with fatigue. "The guns…" he whispered, his voice rough. "They've stopped?"

"For now," Anna said softly. "You're safe."

He blinked, trying to focus on her face. "You were there. Last night."

"I was." She smiled faintly. "You gave us quite a battle yourself."

A ghost of a grin tugged at his lips. "You won, I think."

"I usually do."

He gave a low chuckle that turned into a hiss of pain. She reached to steady him, one hand at his shoulder. "Lie still," she said gently. "You've lost a lot of blood."

"I've had worse," he murmured, though the pallor in his face betrayed the bravado. His fingers brushed weakly at the blanket. "How long…"

"Just the night," she said. "You've been sleeping. The doctor says if the wound doesn't fester, you'll walk again."

He turned his head toward her, eyes searching hers. "And you? You look like you haven't slept in a week."

Anna hesitated, caught off guard by the question. Most soldiers didn't notice her exhaustion; they barely noticed her at all. "We all do what we must," she said simply.

He studied her for a long moment before closing his eyes. "You have a kind voice," he murmured.

The words were so soft she almost thought she'd imagined them. She dipped the cloth again, cooling his skin. Outside, the first rays of morning crept through the seams of the tent, turning the dust in the air to motes of gold.

A nurse passed behind her, whispering, "He'll live?"

Anna nodded without turning. "Ja. He'll live."

When Lukas stirred again, she offered him a sip of water. He reached for the cup, his hand trembling. She guided it to his lips.

"Danke," he said quietly. The corners of his mouth curved. "Anna," he whispered, tasting the name as though it anchored him to something beyond pain and war.

For a moment, the noise of the world seemed to fall away. The morning light brightened, touching his face, revealing the youth beneath the grime and fatigue. He looked impossibly young to have seen so much death.

Anna wrung out the cloth again, her movements slow and deliberate. "Rest, Lukas," she whispered. "You're safe now."

He closed his eyes, his breathing evening out, and she sat beside him for a long while—listening not to the silence, but to the fragile sound of life returning.

The days that followed blurred into one another—gray skies, the scent of antiseptic, and the unending rhythm of bandages changed, fevers tended, and letters written for those too weak to hold a pen.

But amid the unrelenting routine, something gentle began to take root.

* * *

The first nights were the hardest. Lukas drifted in and out of fever, his face pale, his breath ragged. Anna sat at his bedside longer than her shift required, dabbing his forehead with cool water, murmuring reassurances in German and sometimes slipping into Yiddish when her heart ached too much to hold the words in.

Once, when the fever broke, she found his eyes on her. Clear, steady, though tired.
"You never leave me," he said hoarsely.

Anna smiled faintly, tucking the blanket closer around his chest. "You notice too much for a man who should be sleeping."

A ghost of a laugh escaped him, though it quickly turned into a wince of pain.
"Sleep comes easier when you are near," he admitted, surprising them both.

Her hand lingered at his brow for a heartbeat longer than necessary. She had promised herself never to blur the line between nurse and patient, but Lukas's words tugged at something inside her — a thread of warmth in the midst of so much coldness and loss.

CHAPTER TWO:
Prayers

But no day near the front ever finished with anything so simple. The ward filled again as the night deepened. Anna moved through it, steady, precise: pulse, breath, fever, morphine for one, nothing for the man who had already taken too much. Now and then, she returned to Lukas, who drifted in and out of sleep like a boat untethered. Toward dawn, when the lamps were low and the cold flowed in under the tent flaps, she sat a moment in the chair at his bedside and closed her eyes. Her lips moved soundlessly. The old words rose without effort: *Baruch atah Adonai...* Blessed are You, Lord our God—words for breath, for morning, for mercy.

When she opened her eyes, Lukas was watching her.

"A prayer?" he asked, voice no more than air.

"A habit," she said. Something in her chest tightened, the familiar calculus of what to share and what to guard. She softened it with a small smile. "And a comfort."

He nodded, as if those two could be separated, and slept.

Recovery was a stretch of stubborn days. The wound refused to heal as fast as either of them wanted. Fever flirted and retreated, his leg bound tight and propped on a stack of folded linens—but he was alive, and that was more than many could say. In the first few days, he spoke little. Pain and morphine made conversation a fogged thing. But as the fever broke, his voice returned—low, rough-edged, yet threaded with quiet humor.

There were good days, when Lukas sat propped on pillows and ate the broth she coaxed on him, and bad days, when he fell asleep mid-sentence and she changed his dressing with the quick care of someone who knew how quickly flesh could turn against itself.

They learned each other's measures in the small ways that pass between nurse and patient when the days were too long. He liked his water cold; he disliked being left in silence with his thoughts. He stifled groans because the man in the next bed had worse to bear. He twisted his wedding band—only there was none, Anna realized, only the habit of a hand that once returned to a certain place to be sure of what it knew. He was not married. He reached for certainty anyway.

"Your family?" she asked one afternoon as she rewrapped the bandage, her fingers quick, the knot neat.

"Farmers," he said. "My brother Karl is out there somewhere." He flicked his eyes toward the horizon, as if the trenches lay just beyond the canvas. "I volunteered first. I thought—I thought one of us would be enough."

"And now?"

"Now I think there isn't enough of anything." He rubbed his face and gave her a short, embarrassed laugh. "Forgive me. It's difficult to be—"

"Alive?" she offered.

He glanced up at her. "Ja."

Anna tied the last knot. She sat back on her heels and folded the used bandage into the basin. "You are allowed to be complicated, Herr Schneider," she said. "Only the dead are simple."

* * *

"Do you ever grow used to it?" Lukas asked one afternoon, his gaze fixed on the pale canvas ceiling above.

"The war?" she replied.

He nodded faintly.

"No," she said. "You learn to work through it, but it never stops echoing inside you."

He studied her face then, his eyes sharp even through the haze of pain. "You sound like someone who's seen too much."

"I've seen enough." She gave a small, sad smile. "But not as much as you."

He looked down at his leg—the clean dressing stark against his skin. "It doesn't feel like it belongs to me anymore," he admitted. "As if part of me is still out there… in that mud."

Anna paused, her hand resting lightly on his knee. "Perhaps it's not lost," she said softly. "Perhaps you've only left it behind for now. Sometimes we must leave pieces of ourselves to survive."

He regarded her in silence for a moment, then nodded, his expression thoughtful. "You speak like a poet, not a nurse."

"Poets don't last long in war," she replied.

A shadow crossed his face. "Nor soldiers."

They fell quiet. Outside, distant gunfire rumbled— muted but relentless, like thunder on the horizon. The war was never far; it simply waited for its next chance to roar.

Later that evening, when the lamps had been turned low, she found him awake again. The tent had quieted—just the soft

30

breaths of the wounded and the distant whimper of a man dreaming of battle.

"Could you read something?" he asked.

She hesitated, surprised. "What would you like?"

"Anything. I want to hear your voice say something that isn't about blood or pain."

Anna glanced toward her small cot by the supply chest, where her mother's worn prayer book lay. She picked it up, thumbed through the yellowed pages, and began to read—not scripture, but a poem scribbled in the margins long ago by her father.

Her voice was low, warm as candlelight.
It spoke of home—of chestnut trees and the scent of bread at dusk, of children's laughter echoing through narrow streets.

When she finished, Lukas was quiet for a long while. Then he whispered, "That sounds like where I grew up."

"Where was that?"

"Bavaria. Near the river. My mother used to bake on Sundays. You could smell the bread halfway down the road." He smiled faintly, eyes distant. "Do you think she still does?"

Anna hesitated, then reached for his hand—lightly, carefully. "I hope she does. I think the world would fall apart faster if mothers stopped baking bread."

That made him laugh—a soft, hoarse sound that broke the stillness like birdsong after rain.

Days turned to weeks. Lukas's strength returned slowly. He began to sit up for meals, to tease the orderlies, to ask for stories of the other patients. And sometimes, when the guns grew loud again, Anna found herself standing a little closer to his cot, as if his presence made the noise bearable.

One gray morning, as she adjusted the splint on his leg, Lukas watched her quietly.

"You don't belong here," he said.

Anna looked up, startled. "What do you mean?"

"This place… this war. You look like someone who used to laugh."

Her breath caught. "Used to?"

He smiled gently. "I think you still could."

She didn't answer. Not right away. But as she tied off the bandage and the wind outside rustled the canvas, she realized she was smiling. Faintly. Against her will.

Outside, the guns rumbled again—closer this time. The sky was heavy, the air tense. But within the narrow world of that tent, amid the clatter of basins and the scent of disinfectant, two souls had begun, quietly, to find one another.

* * *

Some days later, when she brought him a cup of barley coffee so thin it was almost transparent, he asked suddenly, "What were you saying that morning—when it was almost day?"

"What morning?"

"When I woke, and you were moving your lips. A prayer."

"Oh." She set the cup into his hands, felt the tremble there, whether from weakness or something else. "Shacharit. Morning prayer."

He repeated the word clumsily. "Shacharit."

"Ja."

He looked at her for a long moment. "You are—Jewish."

She held his gaze. "Ja."

The silence between them felt like the second before a shell fell. Then Lukas nodded, once, the gesture awkward. His ears reddened. "I… have not known many Jews." He groped for words and found none that did not taste of someone else's church.

Anna began to speak, then stopped. She set the bowl of water on the crate they used as a table. "We can start with barley coffee," she said. "That is what we share."

He produced a rueful smile, relief loosening his features. "Then let us hate barley coffee together."

"Passionately."

They both laughed, soft and surprised, as if something had let go inside the tent.

After that, the talk came easier. Lukas told her about the small white church in his village and the cherry trees in spring, the way the bells sounded when the fog lay low in the valley.

Anna shared the pale blue view from her parents' kitchen window, the way her mother sang to the dough while kneading bread, her father's quiet habit of blessing the children on Friday night with a hand that smelled of lamp oil and ink.

"Your father is a teacher?" Lukas asked.

"A reader," Anna said, choosing the word as if it were a bandage. "He keeps accounts for the shopkeepers. He writes letters for those who cannot. He knows where to find a loaf of bread when there is none."

Lukas looked down at the blanket. "Those are good things," he said, as if naming them could protect them.

"They are," Anna agreed.

* * *

The morning it began, the light was wrong.

It filtered through the canvas in sharp, flickering bursts instead of the pale, steady gray they'd grown used to. The ground trembled before the sound reached them—a low, rolling growl that built until it became a roar.

Anna froze, her hand midway to a basin of fresh water. Outside, shouts rose—first one, then many. Orders barked, boots pounding, horses screaming. Then came the unmistakable sound of artillery—closer than it had been in weeks.

"God help us," whispered the orderly beside her.

The first shell landed less than a hundred meters away. The shockwave made the tent walls billow inward, lanterns swaying wildly from their hooks. Glass shattered somewhere to

34

the left. The air was filled with dust and the acrid scent of smoke.

"Everyone down!" shouted the doctor. "Get the wounded ready for evacuation! Move, move!"

Chaos erupted. Nurses ran for supplies, grabbing what they could. The moans of the injured rose like a terrible chorus as men were lifted from cots and placed on stretchers. Someone screamed as another shell hit, closer still, rattling the metal trays and sending a rain of dirt from the roof seams.

Anna's heart slammed in her chest. She turned—Lukas was half upright in his cot, his face white with effort, one hand gripping the edge as though ready to stand.

"No!" she cried, rushing to him. "You can't walk on that leg yet!"

He looked at her, jaw set. "They'll be overrun. I won't stay here to die in a bed."

"You'll die faster out there!"

He shook his head, defiance burning through the pain. "Then help me, Anna. Please."

The plea in his voice stopped her. She glanced around—the other nurses were already lifting the most critical patients, loading them onto wagons outside. The tent was thinning fast. They didn't have time to argue.

She grabbed his arm. "All right. But you'll do exactly as I say."

He gave a grim nod, teeth clenched as he shifted his weight onto his good leg. She wrapped his arm around her and half-dragged, half-guided him toward the exit. Each step sent a tremor through his body; she could feel his pain through the weight of him.

Outside, the sky was a dull, dirty brown. Smoke rolled across the horizon, where the ridge line trembled with explosions. Shells burst in the distance like monstrous flowers, sending black petals of earth and fire into the air.

The evacuation was chaos—wagons lined up, horses rearing, medics shouting names over the din. The air was filled with the sharp tang of burning fuel and the cries of the wounded.

"Go to the third wagon!" someone yelled. "We're pulling out now!"

Anna tightened her grip on Lukas. "Almost there."

But another explosion tore through the field, so close that the ground bucked beneath them. She stumbled, dragging him down with her as shrapnel whistled through the air. Canvas from a nearby tent went up in flames.

"Anna!" Lukas shouted, throwing his body over hers as debris rained down.

For a moment, all sound vanished—only the ringing in her ears and the thunder in her chest. Then, slowly, the world came back in fragments: the groans of the wounded, the crackle of fire, the frantic voices of men shouting for help.

She blinked, finding Lukas's face inches from hers. His cheek was streaked with soot, a thin line of blood running down from his temple.

"Are you hurt?" he demanded.

She shook her head, dazed. "No… I don't think—"

Another boom, closer still.

He tightened his grip. "We have to move!"

Together they staggered upright, leaning on each other. They stumbled through smoke and chaos, dodging wreckage and fallen men until they reached the wagon line. The driver—his cap askew, eyes wide with fear—was shouting that they were full.

"There's no room!" he cried. "Next one!"

Anna's pulse pounded in her ears. She turned, coughing through the smoke. "Lukas—can you make it to the next wagon?"

He nodded, though his face was pale as chalk.

They started forward again. Behind them, another shell landed, and the air burst into fire. Anna felt the heat on her back, heard the scream of a horse, the collapse of a burning tent.

Then—through the chaos—she saw it: the last wagon, its canvas torn, but empty enough for one more. She half-dragged Lukas to it. The driver reached down and hauled him in; Anna climbed after.

The moment she clutched the edge, the wagon lurched forward. Wheels thundered through mud, hooves splashing through the churned earth.

Anna turned to look back—behind them, the hospital tents were burning, their white fabric glowing orange against the smoky dawn.

Beside her, Lukas gripped her hand. "You saved me again," he said quietly.

Anna met his eyes, her throat tightening. "No," she whispered. "We saved each other."

The wagon jolted onward, away from the collapsing line, the sky behind them red and black and roaring. And as they fled through the broken countryside, Anna realized that the war was not done with them yet—but neither, it seemed, were they done with hope.

* * *

The wagon wheels ground to a halt long after the sun had risen. The ride had been brutal—mud, ruts, jolting over broken earth—but now, at last, they stopped. The air was heavy with the sour smell of smoke and damp canvas. The field station was little more than a scattering of tents hastily erected on a patch of churned grass near a copse of leafless trees.

Anna climbed down first, her legs unsteady. Around her, medics and orderlies hurried to unload the wounded, their faces drawn tight with exhaustion and grief. The wounded groaned softly; the horses stamped and snorted, their hides streaked with mud.

"Here," she called to two stretcher-bearers, gesturing to Lukas, who was trying—stubbornly—to climb down on his own.

"I can walk," he muttered.

"You can barely stand," she said, her tone sharper than she intended.

He met her gaze and, after a pause, gave a small, rueful smile. "You're a difficult nurse."

"And you," she replied, "are a terrible patient."

38

But the moment her eyes softened, he stopped resisting. He allowed the bearers to lower him gently to the ground and carry him inside.

The new medical tent was smaller—crowded already with rows of wounded men. The air was thick with antiseptic and the low murmur of voices. Anna followed Lukas to an empty cot near the back, where the light came through the canvas in pale streaks.

When they laid him down, she adjusted his blanket, smoothing it carefully around his shoulders. His breathing was labored but even. The bandage around his thigh was damp; she'd have to change it soon.

"You should rest," she said quietly.

He looked up at her. "And you?"

"I don't have that luxury."

Lukas studied her for a long moment. "You haven't stopped since yesterday."

She hesitated, then sat on the edge of his cot. Around them, the sounds of the camp seemed to dim—the voices, the movement, even the steady rumble of distant guns fading into the background.

"I keep thinking about the ones we lost," she murmured. "So many… we couldn't move fast enough."

His expression darkened. "War takes everything. And still asks for more."

Anna's gaze fell to her hands, trembling faintly in her lap. "Sometimes I wonder if it will ever stop asking."

For a moment, neither spoke. A bird called somewhere beyond the trees—thin, uncertain, as if testing whether it was safe to sing again.

Lukas shifted slightly, wincing but managing a faint smile. "Do you remember what you told me? That we must leave pieces of ourselves behind to survive?"

She nodded.

He reached for her hand. "Then let this be one we keep. This—right now."

Anna looked down at his hand over hers—rough, calloused, still warm. The small gesture seemed to bridge something vast and unspeakable between them.

"I'll hold it," she said softly.

He smiled. "Good."

A silence settled between them, not heavy like before but gentle, like a held breath.

When she rose to tend to the next patient, Lukas caught her sleeve. "Anna."

She turned.

"When this is over…" He hesitated, searching her face. "Do you think people like us—who've seen all this—can still find peace?"

Her throat tightened. She wanted to say yes, wanted to promise that there would be peace and quiet fields and the smell of bread again—but the words stuck.

"I don't know," she admitted. "But I think we have to try."

He nodded once, his gaze steady. "Then I'll try. For both of us."

Anna's heart clenched at that—his quiet resolve, so fragile and brave in equal measure. She brushed his hair back from his forehead, the touch tender but fleeting. "Rest now, Lukas."

He closed his eyes, a faint smile still lingering on his lips.

CHAPTER THREE:
Inner Conflict

The night stretched on, every tick of time measured in Lukas's breaths. Anna sat rigid at his side, her fingers wrapped around his, whispering soft words as though they might anchor him to life. But even as her lips spoke comfort, her mind wandered home.

She thought of her parents — the way her father's eyes darted to the window when strangers passed, the way her mother hushed her voice at dusk. She remembered the packages hidden beneath flour sacks, the coded letters slipped into the hands of travelers who never lingered long. The Müllers had chosen their side quietly, in shadows: to help the Allies, to resist in the only way they could.

Anna bore their secret like a second skin. Here, among German officers and soldiers, she could not breathe a word, not to the other nurses, not to the doctors, not even to the men whose lives she tried to save. Least of all to Lukas — and yet it was to him her heart leaned most fiercely.

The dawn was pale, uncertain, much like her own heart. She sat with Lukas's hand clasped in hers, feeling the faint thrum of life return beneath his fevered skin. For a moment, relief surged so strongly she nearly spoke all that was in her— the fear, the prayers, the ache that had grown into something deeper than duty.

But she stopped herself. There was a process to these things: what to share and what to guard. He was still fragile, hovering between worlds. To pour her whole soul into him now might burden him when he needed only rest. And yet, to say nothing left her hollow, aching with words unsaid.

She pressed a cloth to his brow, watching his lips move in a dreamt prayer, or maybe a battlefield cry. How could she tell him the truth of her family, when he wore the very uniform her parents quietly defied? How could she let him close enough to see her whole self, when that truth might endanger not only her but those she loved?

The thoughts of what to share and what to guard tore at her as surely as the fever had torn at him. She wanted to whisper everything — her fears, her longings, even the secrets she had carried since childhood. But she stayed silent. The only words she gave him were the safest ones:

"You're not alone. I will not leave you."

That was all—for now. Enough to tether him gently to the world, but not enough to betray the storm inside her. Her secrets would wait until he was stronger, until his eyes opened and truly saw her again.

Her voice cracked, but she steadied it, smoothing his blond hair back as dawn's first light crept into the tent. She held her secret like a stone in her chest, wondering if the day would come when love would demand its unveiling — or if that truth would remain forever guarded, even from the man whose life she was fighting to preserve.

* * *

The war pressed in differently for those who lay still and those who stood moving. Anna's hours were long but predictable: dawn rounds, dressings, injections, the endless hunger of men whose bodies chewed through every calorie to heal. She slipped a piece of bread to the French prisoner who swept the yard and took the scolding when the sister superior caught her. "He is a mouth," the sister said sharply. "We are all mouths." Anna lowered her eyes and nodded, and did it again the next day.

Outside, the wind shifted, carrying the faint scent of rain. The guns were still there, distant but unrelenting—but in that small corner of the world, amid the ruin and loss, there was also something else: the fragile, defiant pulse of hope.

By early spring, the mud had hardened into uneven ruts, and the thawing fields beyond the camp gleamed like dull brass under a weak sun. The days had grown longer, but the sound of war was never far—sometimes distant, like the grumbling of a restless sky, sometimes close enough to rattle the enamel basins on the shelves.

Inside the field station, Anna moved briskly between cots, sleeves rolled up, hair pinned beneath her cap. Her hands were deft, her voice calm—but beneath the practiced rhythm of her work was a pulse of quiet dread. The front had shifted again. The wounded arriving now came with stories of the enemy pushing closer by the hour.

Lukas gained strength. He was walking again—slowly, with crutches and a stubborn refusal to rest. His uniform had been mended, his face still pale but stronger now, the lines of pain replaced by resolve.

He walked to the door on his crutches and stood looking at the sky as if astonished that it could be blue. One evening, the orderlies wheeled him to the little garden behind the wards, where winter cabbages struggled up from stiff earth. The air smelled of damp and woodsmoke; somewhere a lark sang, mad with its own defiance. Anna sat with him on a bench and drew her shawl around her shoulders.

"You shouldn't be out here," Anna called softly. "You'll undo all the work I did putting you back together."

He turned, the faintest smile tugging at his mouth. "You did too good a job for that. I can't lie in that cot forever, Anna."

She joined him, folding her arms as she looked out toward the fields. "You shouldn't be standing either."

"I have to try." His hand tightened around the cane. "If the front reaches us again, I need to be ready."

Anna frowned. "You're still recovering. You can barely walk half a mile."

He looked down at her, his gray-blue eyes steady. "Then I'll walk a half mile if that's all I can give."

Her breath caught at the quiet conviction in his tone. He wasn't speaking of duty anymore. He was speaking of survival—of a need to *do something*, anything, to reclaim a piece of himself that the war had nearly taken.

For a long moment, they stood side by side in the thin sunlight, the air carrying the faint hum of distant artillery.

"You should be resting," he said.

"Then sit with me while I disobey."

He grinned. In that moment he looked younger than he was, the lines of pain eased by something like hope. "If we are to be criminals," he said, "we should at least do something scandalous."

"Like what?"

"Like, talk honestly," he said, and his smile went crooked.

She studied his face, the healing softness around his mouth. "All right."

He was quiet for a long time. "I believed it would be glorious," he said finally. "The posters, the banners, the priest's hand on my head. I believed the Kaiser loved us and God would not let so many of us die for nothing."

"And now?"

"I try not to ask God about it," he said, a miserable little laugh under the words. "I am ashamed to think I knew so little of pain."

Anna let the silence stand with them. Then she said, "When I was a child, my mother told me: pain is uninvited, but you can decide whether it is a thief or a teacher."

Lukas looked at her. "And this?"

"This is a thief," she said simply. "And we will not let it take more than it must."

He reached for her hand, hesitated, and let his fingers rest on the bench between them. "You make it seem possible," he said.

"It is not my work to make it seem anything," Anna said, her voice very soft. "Only to witness. And to bandage. And to not grow hard."

The wind moved the kitchen garden's dry leaves. He turned his face toward her. In the dull light, his eyes were silver.

"I do not want to grow hard either," he said.

They walked back slowly. At the tent flap, he stopped. "Anna," he said, and she looked at him and felt, with a shock, how wholly her name already belonged in his mouth.

46

"Yes?"

He swallowed. "If I… If I leave—"

"You will heal," she said, too quickly, not wanting him to finish the sentence. "You will go home."

"Or back to the line," he said, honest. "If that happens, will you—would you—remember me?"

Her breath caught. She had thought herself careful. "I will," she said, the words simple as a vow. "And you will remember there is someone in a white cap who is very stubborn on your behalf." She sighed, not wanting to think what might happen. "You'll be sent back to your unit soon," she said at last.

"I know."

"Do you want to go back?"

He hesitated. "Want?" He shook his head. "No. But men I know are still out there. If they can face it, so can I."

Anna swallowed hard. "And if I asked you not to?"

He looked at her then—not as a patient, not as a soldier, but as a man seeing the woman who had held his life in her hands. "Would you?"

Her lips parted, but no words came. She turned away, her pulse hammering. "It doesn't matter what I want."

"Ja," he said quietly. "It does. I will come back."

A gust of wind stirred the loose edges of her apron. She closed her eyes, steadying herself. "Lukas… you shouldn't make promises in a war. They never survive."

"Then let me make one that will," he said. "If I go back, I'll come find you when it's over. No matter how far I have to walk."

Her throat ached. "You might not come back at all."

He leaned closer, close enough that she could feel the warmth of him, smell the faint trace of smoke and soap on his skin. "And you might never know if I tried."

Their eyes met—his fierce, hers shining with everything she couldn't say. Somewhere nearby, a shell rumbled in the distance, a reminder that even in stillness, the war breathed.

She broke the silence first, whispering, "You should rest before the next transport comes."

He caught her hand as she turned to go. "Anna."

She looked back.

"I meant what I said," he told her. "When this ends— whatever's left of the world—I'll find you."

Her hand trembled in his. She didn't trust her voice, so she only nodded once.

He smiled, and it slid into something like pain before it steadied. "Then I will live," he said, as if her promise could buckle his armor.

* * *

The Feldgendarmerie came three days after the rumors began. They entered the ward with the loudness of men who believe silence is disloyal. The officer in front had a square

48

face and a small mustache. He consulted a paper, looked up, and found Anna.

"Fräulein Müller," he said. "You are to come with us."

"On what grounds?" she asked, setting a tray of syringes carefully on a metal table.

"Questioning," he said. "We have reports of food and messages passed to prisoners."

Anna felt every eye in the ward. She looked automatically to the sister superior, who spoke quickly, too quickly: "She is a good nurse, Lieutenant. Surely—"

"Surely the Fatherland cannot be undone by a nurse," the lieutenant said dryly. "Nevertheless."

Anna undid her apron and folded it in thirds. Her heart thudded, foolishly fast. She had made such small choices—a crust pressed into a palm, a letter passed from one hand to another, a nod at the wrong time to the wrong man. Small things, each so human they barely seemed like choices. And yet here she was.

Lukas swung his legs off the bed. He was on crutches and pale, but he crossed the short distance as if the ground were on fire. "Herr Lieutenant," he said. "A moment."

The officer turned to him, unimpressed. "You are not on the roster to stand," he snapped.

"I am on the roster to speak," Lukas said, jaw tight. "Fräulein Müller is my nurse. Any contact she has with prisoners has been under my direction as a patient's escort to the yard. If there has been impropriety, it is mine."

Anna felt heat rise to her cheeks and then drop as quickly, like a fever breaking. She wanted to close his foolish, brave mouth with her hand. The lieutenant studied Lukas, then flicked his gaze to Anna. Something complicated moved across his face—boredom, impatience, the calculation of trouble against paperwork.

"Is that so?" he said.

"It is," Lukas said. "I will sign a statement. Or you may take me instead."

"You," the lieutenant said, "would not get past the first door." He sighed, as if the morning had already been too long. "See that you keep your nurse to her work." He crumpled the paper in his hand with performative indifference. "Fräulein Müller, consider yourself warned."

They left. The ward breathed again, in the jagged way of a flock that has seen the hawk pass and not strike. Anna turned to Lukas, anger and relief sparring in her chest.

"You fool," she whispered. "What if he had decided to make an example?"

"Then we would both have learned whether I am as brave as I wish to be," he said, and in spite of everything, she almost laughed.

She reached for his arm, steadying him. He leaned into her touch, and she felt his tremble and did not pretend it was only weakness.

"Thank you," she said.

"I owed you more than a prayer," he said softly.

CHAPTER FOUR:
Good-byes

Spring came smelling of thaw and rot. With it came orders. Lukas's chart bore a neat note in the surgeon's hand: Fit for duty with light limitations. That night, they went to the garden again because there was nowhere else to go to say what could not be said in a tent full of ears.

"I will write," Lukas said, a promise too big to live unhurt in the world. "Censors be damned."

"You will not write where you are," Anna said. "You will write who you are." She touched the sleeve of his jacket where a careful seamstress had mended the worst of it. "Tell me about your church bells. Tell me how the light is in the morning on the barn door."

"I will tell you that your name tastes like water after salt," he blurted, as if the sentence had escaped him.

Her eyes stung. "And I will tell you that the cabbages are growing," she said, trying to manage a smile.

He stepped closer on his ruined leg, the cane tucked under his arm forgotten. He stood with his breath shaking. "Anna."

"Yes."

"May I?" he asked, like a boy at a door.

She answered with her mouth on his. It was not a practiced kiss, not something stolen by skill; it was two people startled by how quickly a need could find its hand and take what it wanted. His hand cupped the back of her head as if she were hurt and he could hold her safe. She tasted salt and barley and the iron of blood that had no story anymore. When they parted, they were both breathing as if they had run a long way.

"This is foolish," she said, the words trembling.

"It is the first true thing," he said.

They did not speak much after that. The night thinned to a grayness that made the tents look like ships on a cold sea.

* * *

That night, when the wounded slept and the lamps burned low, Anna sat at her small desk and wrote her name carefully across the back of a ration slip. Beneath it, she added a single line:

If you live—come to Heidelberg. The house with the chestnut tree still stands.

She slipped it into Lukas's pack while he slept.

* * *

The next morning, orders came down. The front had moved again, and all able-bodied soldiers were being sent forward.

That day, he rose from his cot, and Anna's heart clenched. He still walked stiffly, the deep scar along his thigh tugging with each step, but he carried himself with the quiet pride of a man unwilling to be broken. His uniform hung looser than before, patched at the knee where blood and mud had ruined it, but he had polished his boots himself that morning, as if the small act could restore some sense of dignity.

Anna watched from the flap of the tent as he tightened the strap on his kit and shouldered his rifle again. The sun glinted off the steel, and for a moment she saw not just a soldier but the boyish resolve beneath the hardened lines of his face.

"You're not ready," she said softly when he passed near her.

He paused, meeting her eyes. There was warmth there, gratitude that words could not hold, but also the iron will of a man who knew his duty. "No one here is ready, Fräulein Müller," he replied, voice low. "But I cannot lie in that bed while others bleed."

Her throat tightened. She wanted to tell him her secret — about her parents, about the dangerous path her family had chosen. But again, she kept it close. Instead, she stepped forward and adjusted the strap of his pack, her fingers lingering for just a moment on his shoulder.

"Then promise me," she whispered. "Promise me you will come back."

He held her gaze a long time, as if weighing what he could give against what the war might take. Finally, he nodded, a vow made without flourish, but one that carried the weight of truth.

He limped toward the departing column, cane in hand. He turned once at the edge of the yard, lifted his cane in an awkward salute. She raised her hand. Then he was gone, striding toward the column of men, the thunder of distant guns already calling him forward.

Anna stood at the edge of the road, her heart lodged somewhere between fear and pride. The guns were already thundering again in the distance, shaking the ground beneath her boots.

And though she didn't know if she'd ever see him again, she whispered to the smoke-dark sky, "Come back to me."

They parted where the ward began, because that was where wars asked people to be small again so others could be fed, dressed, turned, washed. She did not cry until she had three beds to make and could cry into the sheets.

CHAPTER FIVE:
Lukas Returns to Duty

Rain fell in gray sheets as Lukas trudged through the mire of the front, his cane replaced now by a rifle, his leg wrapped tight beneath the soaked wool of his uniform. The world had become mud and smoke, sky and thunder. The air stank of cordite and rot; the trenches were rivers of filth that swallowed men whole.

They'd marched for three days through rain and shellfire to reach this position—a shattered line of sandbags and splintered timbers clinging to the edge of a cratered field. The men around him were ghosts in helmets, faces streaked with grime, eyes hollow. Somewhere, a machine gun rattled, then fell silent.

"Keep your head down!" barked the sergeant, his voice hoarse. "They've sighted the line again!"

Lukas dropped into the trench as another shell landed nearby. The blast tore the air apart, showering them with mud and shards of wood. He pressed himself against the wet wall, heart hammering. When the ringing in his ears subsided, he realized he was still clutching something in his coat pocket— Anna's ration slip.

He drew it out just long enough to glimpse her careful handwriting, the ink slightly blurred from his fingers. *The house with the chestnut tree still stands.*

He folded it again and tucked it safely away. That single scrap of paper was the only warmth he had.

The night that followed was endless. Rain drummed on his helmet; rats skittered along the duckboards. Now and then the horizon would flare with gunfire, and the sound rolled over them like distant thunder. Lukas couldn't tell where the enemy ended and the earth began. Everything was blurred, soaked, trembling.

He remembered her hands—the way they moved swiftly and surely, even when everything around her was chaos. He remembered her voice, low and steady, whispering to men who screamed in pain, anchoring them to life. He remembered the faint scent of lavender soap, the way the lantern light softened the edges of her face.

When the shelling started again near dawn, he pressed his back to the trench and closed his eyes, whispering her name like a prayer.

"Anna."

The man beside him—a boy, really, no older than seventeen—looked up, shivering. "Who's Anna?"

Lukas gave a faint, humorless smile. "Someone worth living for."

The boy stared at him for a moment, then nodded and returned his gaze to the mud.

By midday, the order came. Advance.

They climbed from the trench into a wasteland of churned soil and twisted wire. The air was heavy with smoke, the sky a smear of gray. Men shouted; rifles cracked; the ground erupted in bursts of fire. Lukas moved with the others, his leg aching, his breath short.

Then came the machine guns.

The first volley cut through the line like a scythe. Men fell—some screaming, some simply dropping where they stood. Lukas hit the ground, crawling through the mud, his fingers slipping on the slick earth. He could hear the whine of bullets overhead, the roar of another explosion somewhere to his left.

When he lifted his head, he saw the boy who had asked about Anna lying a few feet away, still, his helmet rolling into a puddle.

For a heartbeat, Lukas froze. Then something inside him hardened—not anger, not even fear, but a fierce, steady resolve. He crawled forward, dragging the boy's body back toward what was left of a trench wall, shielding him from the falling debris even though he knew it was too late.

The world was chaos—men shouting, guns screaming—but through it all, Anna's voice echoed in his mind: *You're safe now. You're safe.*

He knew he wasn't, not really. None of them were. But that memory—her calm, her courage—was something the war couldn't take.

Hours later, when the guns finally went quiet and night fell over the shattered field, Lukas sat against a broken post, his body trembling with exhaustion. He stared up at the dim stars just visible through the drifting smoke.

"I'll come back," he whispered to no one, his voice rough, his breath misting in the cold air. "I'll find you, Anna."

The guns answered with distant thunder, and the wind carried the scent of smoke and rain—like the world itself was holding its breath, waiting to see if men like Lukas could keep such promises.

* * *

The trenches stank of mud, cordite, and men who had lived too long without sleep. Lukas crouched low, his rifle across his knees, boots sunk deep in filth that never dried. The sky above was a strip of slate, torn by the flashes of artillery in the distance. Every blast rattled the boards at his back, every whistling shell sent men ducking instinctively deeper into the earth.

He shifted his weight and winced as his thigh pulled tight around the scar left by the shrapnel. It was healed enough to carry him here, but in the cold, damp, it ached with a dull, gnawing reminder of how close he had come to death. He flexed his hand, remembering another hand that had held his through the fever. Anna's voice whispered at the edges of his thoughts—steady, gentle, coaxing him back to life.

"Hold on," she had said. *"You are not alone."*

A shout tore through the line—*Achtung!*—and Lukas was on his feet, peering over the parapet. Smoke hung over the killing ground like a shroud. Figures moved in it, shadowy and advancing. His stomach twisted, fear rising sharp as bile, but training took over. He fired, the recoil biting into his shoulder, the sound lost in the rolling thunder of guns.

Around him, men yelled, cursed, bled. The trench was chaos—mud flying, bodies falling, the sharp stink of cordite mingling with blood. Lukas ducked as earth rained down from an explosion just beyond the wall, clods stinging his face. For a heartbeat he thought he would never stand again, never draw another breath.

But then he remembered the pale light of dawn in the hospital tent, Anna's tired eyes watching over him, and he forced himself up. For her—for the promise he had given—he would not falter here.

He lifted his rifle once more, the world reduced to mud, smoke, and survival, while somewhere in the back of his mind he clung to the thought of her voice, waiting like a beacon beyond the storm.

The whistle shrieked down the line—a high, keening sound that cut through the thunder of artillery. Men scrambled to the ladders, boots slipping on mud-slick rungs. Lukas felt the shove of bodies pressing close as the order passed down the trench: "Over! Forward! Vorwärts!"

He climbed, lungs burning, the damp air thick with smoke and fear. The moment his head broke above the parapet, the world exploded. Machine-gun fire stitched the ground ahead, throwing up fountains of dirt. He flung himself forward, stumbling into the churned no-man's-land, his rifle tight in his grip.

The ground sucked at his boots with every step, mud mingled with blood, helmets, shattered wood, and the twisted wreckage of lives ended in the last charge. Shells burst ahead, spraying shards of steel and earth. A man to his right crumpled with a cry, the weight of him dragging Lukas sideways before he tore free and pressed on.

"Vorwärts!" the sergeant bellowed again, voice ragged with smoke and command. Lukas obeyed, half-running, half-crawling toward the shadow of the wire. Bullets snapped overhead, whining close. He threw himself flat, breath heaving, his cheek pressed to the cold, stinking mud.

For a moment, panic clawed at him—raw and choking. *Why here? Why now?* His leg throbbed, his chest heaved, the urge to curl into the mud and disappear almost irresistible. But in the roaring din, another memory surfaced: the cool cloth Anna had pressed to his brow, her whispered words when he had been closest to death.

"You are not alone."

He grit his teeth, dug his elbows in, and hauled himself forward inch by inch. Wire snagged at his sleeve, tearing it open, but he forced through, the world narrowing to survival, to the pounding of his heart. Around him, men cried out, some falling silent forever, some calling for their mothers, their God, anyone to hear.

Lukas fired blind toward the line ahead, the recoil jarring through his arms. He thought of his promise—to come back to her, no matter the cost—and it steadied him in a way no officer's command could.

Another shell burst, so close it rattled his bones. The world went white, then deafeningly silent. He blinked, ears ringing, vision blurred, the taste of earth in his mouth. A hand seized his shoulder, dragging him upright—another soldier, mud-streaked and wild-eyed. Together they stumbled forward, into the smoke, into whatever waited beyond.

* * *

The trenches had gone strangely still, the echoes of gunfire replaced by the softer sounds of men settling into their routines. Lukas found himself sitting on an overturned ammunition crate, his back against the packed earth wall, the sharp smell of damp soil and smoke lingering in the air.

Life between battles was made up of small rituals— mending a torn tunic, sharing the last crumbs of bread, or scrawling letters that might never be delivered. In these spaces, friendships took root almost without notice.

He'd grown closest to Matthias, a broad-shouldered farm boy from Saxony who always managed to scrounge extra rations. Matthias had a loud laugh that seemed almost defiant against the war. Then there was Erich, quiet and thoughtful, who carried a battered volume of Goethe's poetry and sometimes read aloud by candlelight. They made an odd trio— Lukas the earnest one, Matthias the boisterous optimist, and Erich the dreamer—but the bond steadied them when the guns grew silent.

At night, they traded stories of home. Matthias spoke of fields that needed plowing, Erich of a girl he hoped would wait for him, and Lukas, hesitating, described his small village and the family dinners he missed. He never told them about the nurse with kind eyes he had only just met—Anna—yet her presence lingered in his thoughts, unspoken but warming.

Friendship in war was fragile, built on laughter stolen between barrages, on the comfort of another's voice in the dark. Lukas found himself clinging to these moments. They made the mud, the waiting, and the uncertainty bearable.

* * *

The barracks smelled of damp wool and pipe smoke, lit only by a flickering lantern swinging from a nail in the beam overhead. Lukas sat cross-legged on the floor with Matthias and Erich, a makeshift table between them—a plank laid over two crates.

Matthias slapped down a card with exaggerated flair. "There! Beat that, eh?" His laugh boomed through the low ceiling.

Erich shook his head, lips twitching as he fished through his hand. "You play like a farmer counting pigs. Loud, but no strategy."

61

Lukas grinned and slid a card into the pile. "Then I suppose it's your pigs against my sheep." He leaned back as Matthias groaned dramatically, tossing his cards down in defeat.

A chorus of jeers and cheers came from the bunks around them as other men leaned in to watch. The game had no prize—only the pleasure of distraction. Still, when Lukas quietly produced a handful of chocolate he'd bartered from a supply cart, the men's eyes widened. He broke the pieces into three and handed them out, a fragile sweetness cutting through the sour taste of war.

* * *

The night was thin and cold, a pale mist curling through the camp. Lukas huddled with Matthias and Erich behind the shadow of a supply tent, passing a dented flask between them.

"From home," Matthias whispered proudly. "My brother smuggled it into a parcel. Don't ask how."

The wine was rough but warming. They drank in silence at first, listening to the distant rumble of artillery. Finally, Erich spoke, voice soft. "Do you ever think about after? What we'll do when this ends?"

Lukas hesitated. He thought of Anna's gentle hands, of her voice like a balm against fever. He didn't speak her name, but something in his silence told the others enough. Matthias clapped him on the shoulder, grinning. "A girl, eh? That's good. Gives you something to fight for."

The flask came back around. They toasted softly—"To home. To surviving. To the morning." The mist thickened, the eastern sky paling with the first touch of dawn. Soon, the orders

62

would come, boots and rifles would rattle again. But for a moment, three young men shared stolen warmth and the illusion of peace.

* * *

Letters came when they could, and when they couldn't, they came in dreams. Lukas wrote on field postcards, lines drawn like trenches. He wrote about frost heaving the duckboards, about a stray cat in the dugout, about a chaplain who sang like a church pew and made the men's mouths quirk even when there was nothing to laugh at.

Once he wrote:" *I will come back"*. Once she wrote: *"I will be where you can find me."*

Winter ground them both thin. The turnips were gray and tasted of the earth; the hospital ration kettles sank in like graves. Men coughed and did not stop. The Feldgendarmerie returned to the village where her parents lived; someone whispered that Herr Müller's ledger contained names that should not appear together. Anna wrote home in careful sentences that said everything without saying anything at all. Her mother's reply smelled of lamp oil and flour: *"We are all right. Keep warm. Trust the small lights."*

Spring came again. Letters slowed, then stuttered to silence. Weeks became a silence that had its own weight. The war wore a new shape—mutinies, rumors, speeches in beer halls that made the sisters cross themselves. In the ward, Anna fed whoever was in front of her. She learned to say the names of places her hands would never touch: *Flanders, Ypres, Cambrai.* At night, she lay in her narrow cot and put the back of her hand over her mouth to keep from making any sound at all.

63

CHAPTER SIX:
The Dawn March

The column of soldiers trudged forward, boots sucking at the wet earth with each step. Breath misted in the cold morning air, rising like smoke from a hundred mouths. The sound of gear clinking, rifles shifting, and the steady thud of marching blended into a rhythm that dulled thought—until Matthias broke it.

"First thing I'll do when I get home," he said loudly enough for a few men nearby to hear, "is eat an entire roast goose by myself. My mother always said I had a stomach like a wolf."

A ripple of chuckles moved through the ranks. Erich shook his head, eyes forward. "And then you'll be sick for three days. Some homecoming."

"What about you, Lukas?" Matthias asked, elbowing him lightly. "What's waiting for you?"

Lukas hesitated. He thought of Anna—her hands cool against his fevered skin, her voice steady in the chaos of the hospital. But that felt too fragile, too private to expose here on the open road. Instead, he answered carefully, "A warm fire. My father's old chair by the hearth. Bread fresh from the oven."

"That's worse than poetry," Matthias teased. "Bread? You could have at least said roast goose."

Erich smiled faintly, adjusting the strap of his rifle. "Bread is better. Bread means peace." His hand brushed the outline of the small book hidden under his tunic. "For me—it will be a quiet room. And someone to read to."

The three fell silent for a time, the clamor of boots and the faint rumble of distant guns filling the gap. Then Lukas said softly, "When we get through this, we should meet again. All of us. No uniforms, no rifles. Just a table, a loaf of bread, and maybe even your goose, Matthias."

"Done," Matthias said at once, grinning. "But I get the drumstick."

"Then I'll bring the wine," Erich added.

The promise hung between them, small and fragile, but it warmed Lukas more than the dawn sun now climbing above the mist. It gave shape to a future he dared not picture alone.

The march wound through sodden fields and broken hedgerows until the horizon thickened with smoke. The sun had risen higher, but it gave no warmth—only a pale light that revealed churned mud, shattered trees, and the faint outlines of trenches ahead.

"Front line," Matthias muttered, his grin fading.

Orders were barked down the column. Packs shifted, rifles clutched tighter. The easy banter of the road drained away, replaced by silence, each man folding into himself. Lukas felt his heartbeat quicken, as if the ground itself pulsed beneath his boots.

A dull *whump* rolled across the distance, followed by another. Artillery. The shells fell short, black geysers of earth rising into the sky. The line stumbled, then steadied. No one needed to be told: this was only the beginning.

They pushed on, feet dragging through mud that sucked and clung. The air stank of cordite and wet clay. The ground seemed alive with the scars of battle—craters, broken wagons, the husk of a farmhouse leaning into ruin.

As they neared the trenches, Lukas glanced at Erich. His friend's lips moved soundlessly, reciting a line of poetry, perhaps, or a prayer. Matthias spat into the mud and rolled his shoulders, trying for bravado, though his eyes darted nervously toward the smoke.

The next shell fell closer, the explosion a crack of thunder that shook the air and rained dirt down over them. Men ducked instinctively, then staggered forward at the sergeant's roar.

Lukas gripped his rifle tighter, his throat dry. He thought of the promises they had made—bread, goose, wine—and clung to them like a shield against the fear rising in his chest.

They reached the lip of the trench, where the smell of sweat, blood, and gun oil thickened. Officers gestured them down, and one by one, the men disappeared into the earth.

The world above roared with gunfire. The fragile dawn march was over.

* * *

The trench walls pressed close, slick with mud, the air heavy with the stench of sweat and gun oil. Lukas crouched with Matthias and Erich, rifles clutched, waiting for the order. The men's breathing filled the silence between the thunder of shells.

"Steady!" a lieutenant barked, his voice rough but trembling at the edges.

The whistle shrieked. The world lurched forward.

Lukas scrambled up the ladder, boots slipping on the sodden wood, his body shoved ahead by the momentum of men surging behind him. The moment he broke into the open air, the roar of artillery swallowed everything. Earth burst around them in geysers of mud and fire.

He ran, legs pumping, rifle clattering against his shoulder. The ground shook beneath each shell. Men screamed—some stumbled and fell, some didn't rise again. Matthias was at his side, face taut with a grim grin, shouting something Lukas couldn't hear. Erich, pale but determined, pushed forward on Lukas's other flank, his mouth moving in a wordless prayer.

Machine-gun fire rattled from the ridge ahead. Bullets whipped through the air like hornets, tearing into men and soil alike. Lukas threw himself into a crater, lungs heaving, mud splattering his face.

Matthias dropped beside him, panting, laughing wildly as if to spit in death's face. "Goose dinner might have to wait, eh?" he shouted over the din.

Erich stumbled in next, clutching his rifle so tightly his knuckles were bloodless. "Stay low," he gasped, eyes wide but burning with resolve.

Another shell landed close, the concussion slamming into Lukas's chest, rattling his bones. Dirt rained down, stinging his skin. He coughed, spat mud, and forced himself upright.

The whistle blew again, urging them onward.

The crater offered no safety for long. Another whistle, another shove forward—the weight of command heavier than the rifle in Lukas's hands. Lukas met his friends 'eyes— Matthias's reckless grin, Erich's pale determination—and nodded. Together, they climbed from the crater and charged into the storm, the fragile promises of bread, goose, and wine burning like embers in Lukas's heart.

* * *

He hauled himself up, boots slipping on the churned earth, and the battlefield opened before him like a nightmare.

The enemy lines were only a few dozen paces away, a blur of gray shapes moving in smoke and muzzle flashes. Machine-gun fire scythed the air. Men fell around him, their cries drowned beneath the thunder of the guns.

Lukas raised his rifle, hands trembling. He spotted a figure in the haze—another young man, no older than himself, scrambling behind a shattered post. Their eyes met for a heartbeat, wide and startled.
Lukas pulled the trigger.

The rifle kicked hard against his shoulder. The crack echoed inside his skull. The other soldier jerked backward, arms flailing, and disappeared into the mud.

For a moment, the world tilted, as if the ground itself rejected what he'd done. Lukas's stomach heaved; bile burned his throat. He wanted to look away, to unsee—but there was no room for hesitation.

Matthias's hand clamped on his back, steadying him. "Keep moving!" he shouted, eyes wild but alive. "Don't stop now!"

Erich fired beside them, his face ghostly pale, his lips still shaping words Lukas could not hear.

The air stank of sulphur, blood, and churned earth. Lukas stumbled forward, firing again, each shot tearing another piece from him. His ears rang, his vision narrowed. The enemy were no longer shapes in smoke—they were boys, faces flashing in the strobe of fire, falling as quickly as they appeared.

Somewhere in the madness, Lukas realized his heart no longer raced for survival alone. It hammered with the memory of a promise—bread, goose, wine—and the fragile hope of returning to Anna's steady hands, to something human again.

The charge rolled forward in fits and starts, men stumbling through mud pocked with fire and craters. Lukas barely felt his legs—only the pounding of his heart, the dull ache in his shoulder from the rifle's recoil, the metallic taste of blood where he had bitten his tongue.

Matthias surged ahead like a wild bull, yelling over the din, rifle fixed with bayonet. He slashed the air more to keep courage burning than to strike. Erich clung close to Lukas, his lips still moving in half-prayer, half-poem, though the words vanished under the shriek of shells.

They reached the first tangle of barbed wire, bodies strewn across it like broken dolls. The sergeant screamed for cutters. Lukas dropped to his knees, fumbling with the wire, hands slick with mud. Bullets snapped overhead. A man beside him was struck and toppled, crimson blooming across his tunic.

"Faster!" Matthias bellowed, shoving his bayonet into the wire and wrenching it free. The path opened. The whistle blew again.

They stormed across the final stretch. Machine guns raked them, tearing men down in sprays of dirt and blood. Lukas felt something hot and sharp graze his arm—burning, but not enough to stop him. He pressed on, mouth open, lungs screaming.

The enemy trench loomed—shadows of men firing wildly from within. Matthias vaulted first, plunging down with a roar. Lukas followed, boots slipping on the earthen wall, crashing into the pit of chaos.

It was close-quarters now. Bayonets, rifle butts, fists. Lukas's world shrank to flashes of faces, the grunt of blows, the stink of sweat and cordite. He thrust, blocked, swung—moving more from terror than skill. A figure lunged at him; he fired point-blank. The body crumpled.

Then—silence. Not full silence, but the lull that follows madness: groans of the wounded, the crack of a distant rifle, the sergeant's ragged voice calling men to hold.

The trench was theirs.

Lukas collapsed against the wall, chest heaving. His hands shook so violently that he dropped his rifle. Blood smeared his sleeve—not his own, he realized with a sick lurch, but someone else's.

Matthias stumbled into view, face streaked with grime, grinning like a madman. "Told you we'd make it! Goose dinner for us yet!" He was limping, his leg cut and bleeding, but still alive.

Erich sat slumped nearby, his rifle across his knees. His eyes were hollow, shock tightening every line of his face. His book of poetry was gone, lost somewhere in the mud. He met Lukas's gaze and whispered hoarsely, "We killed them all."

Lukas wanted to answer, but his throat locked. He pressed his shaking hands against his knees, forcing breath in and out. Around them, men moved like shadows—dragging the wounded, checking for survivors, piling bodies like cordwood.

The promise of bread, goose, and wine flickered through Lukas's mind like a lantern in the dark. It felt impossibly far away, yet it was the only thing that kept the weight of what he had done from crushing him entirely.

For the first time, Lukas understood: survival was victory enough. And survival came at a cost that would never leave him.

CHAPTER SEVEN:
Quiet in the Dark

The trench stank of iron, of fresh blood mingled with the older rot of mud and death. The ground was slick beneath Lukas's boots, churned by boots and bodies alike. He forced himself not to look too long at the faces of the fallen—they were too young, too much like his own.

Matthias leaned against the wall, his pants torn open at the thigh where the bullet had grazed him. He laughed low, breathless, though the sound bordered on a sob. "Alive. Can you believe it? Still alive." His hands shook as he fumbled for a strip of cloth to bind the wound.

Erich sat beside him, knees drawn up, his rifle lying forgotten in the muck. His lips trembled, his eyes glassy, but his voice carried a terrible clarity. "I thought I would be ready. That was when the time came, I could do it." He looked down at his bloodied hands. "But it was not like I imagined."

Lukas lowered himself into the mud between them, his body aching with exhaustion. "None of us imagined this," he said hoarsely. He tried to wipe his hands clean on his tunic, but the blood smeared darker.

For a moment, the three sat together, silent but bound by something stronger than words. Around them, officers shouted, men dragged the wounded to shelter, and distant guns growled across the fields. Yet in this hollowed-out space, it was only them—their breath misting in the cold air, their eyes haunted by what they had seen and done.

Matthias broke the silence first. "When this war ends—and it will, someday—I'm still roasting that goose. You two are both invited."

Erich let out a thin, brittle laugh. "Bread and goose," he murmured, shaking his head. "God help us if we ever taste it again."

Lukas pressed his back against the earthen wall, staring at the pale strip of sky above the trench. His heart still thundered, but not from fear now—from the knowledge that he had crossed some line he could never step back from. He had taken life, and in doing so, something in him had been taken too.

Still, when he glanced at Matthias's grin, cracked though it was, and at Erich's trembling hands clutched tight as if to hold onto sanity, he felt the thread between them tighten. Fragile, yes, but alive.

And in that moment—against the ruin, the mud, and the stink of death—Lukas clung to it. Because it was all they had left.

* * *

The guns had fallen silent, though the ground still seemed to hum with their echo. Darkness pressed close, broken only by the faint orange glow of lanterns and the occasional flare arcing across the sky. The trench was quiet save for the groans of the wounded and the restless shifting of men too weary to sleep.

Lukas sat wedged between Matthias and Erich, the three huddled together beneath a rough canvas thrown across the trench wall. The air was bitterly cold, and their breath rose in pale plumes.

Matthias was half-dozing, his wounded leg stretched out, bandaged with strips torn from his own tunic. He snored softly between ragged breaths, but even asleep his hand remained curled around his bayonet, as if he dared the darkness to try him.

Erich was awake, eyes reflecting the lantern glow. His hands were clasped as though in prayer, but no words came now. He only stared ahead, lips pressed tight. Lukas followed his gaze, saw the outline of a fallen man in the mud just beyond the firelight, and looked quickly away.

A scrap of bread passed down the trench reached them. Lukas broke it into three pieces, though Matthias was too far gone to notice. He placed one chunk in Erich's palm. "Eat," he whispered.

Erich hesitated, then took a slow bite. "It tastes of ash," he murmured, but finished it all the same.

Lukas chewed his piece, the dry crust catching in his throat. He closed his eyes and tried to summon the image of Anna's face, her steady hands, the promise of something human beyond this pit of mud and blood. For a fleeting moment, warmth flickered through him.

"Tomorrow, or the day after, they'll send us again," Erich said quietly, his voice so low Lukas barely heard.

"Then we go together," Lukas answered, forcing conviction into the words. "Like today. Together."

Erich looked at him, searching his face, and finally gave a small, weary nod.

Matthias stirred, mumbling in his sleep—something about roast goose, the words broken but unmistakable. Lukas almost smiled, the sound a fragile ember in the cold.

The three of them sat in silence as the night deepened, bound by exhaustion, fear, and the promises they dared to whisper into the dark.

The trench breathed with low murmurs and the occasional cough, but for Lukas, time had slowed to the rhythm of their small circle. The lantern's glow softened until it was little more than a trembling star against the black.

Matthias shifted, his head tipping onto Lukas's shoulder, his breath warm and uneven. Erich sat close on the other side, hands still clenched but his eyes finally heavy, lids drooping. For once, he wasn't whispering poems or prayers—only resting, as if silence itself might keep them whole.

Lukas wrapped his arms tighter around himself and let the weight of his friends press in. The cold seeped through his uniform, the mud bit at his boots, but between them a thin shelter formed—something that belonged to no army, no command, only to three boys who had survived the day.

Above, the sky stretched wide and empty, pierced now and then by a distant flare. Lukas watched the light fade, then leaned his head back against the trench wall. His mind flickered between the faces of the dead, the roar of guns, and the faraway thought of Anna's steady hands. He clung hardest to the last.

Matthias murmured again in his sleep, words Lukas could barely catch: "home… goose…"

A weak smile touched Lukas's lips. He closed his eyes, the noise of the day settling into a low hum in his bones. The three of them, pressed shoulder to shoulder, let exhaustion claim them at last.

In the heart of a war-torn night, they found their only refuge—in each other.

* * *

Cold light seeped over the lip of the trench, turning frost to a dull glitter on the sandbags. A whistle—not the kind that sent men over the top, but the short, sharp call of routine—cut through the grey.

"Stand to! Roll call!"

Lukas woke with a start, Matthias's weight still on his shoulder, Erich's sleeve pressed to his. For a second, he didn't know where he was. Then the smell of damp earth and old smoke returned, and the night folded itself away.

They pulled themselves upright. Matthias hissed as his grazed thigh protested, then forced a grin. "Still here."

Erich didn't speak. He wiped at his eyes once, briskly, and fell into the thin line of men as names were read out. The sergeant's voice carried down the trench in clipped syllables. Every answer "Here!" loosened something in Lukas's chest. Every silence tightened it again.

Two names drew no reply.

"Confirm," the sergeant said evenly. A pair of men nodded and moved off toward the far bay to make sure what everyone already knew.

Rations came—lukewarm coffee with a sheen of something on top, a heel of bread, a smear of grease that passed for meat. Lukas handed half his bread to Matthias without comment, and Matthias took it without thanks, both favors understood. Erich held his tin mug in both hands as if it were something sacred, steaming his face, saying nothing.

Orders filtered down like bad weather.

"Repair party to B Company's forward wall. You, you, and you—" a corporal's finger hopped along the line, landed on Lukas. "Bring your shovels. Wire party at the second stand to follow. Medics expect stretcher work—rotations on the hour."

Lukas nodded, the motion automatic. His muscles felt older than he was, his shoulder bruised to the bone from yesterday's firing. He cleaned his rifle anyway, field-stripping on the plank of a duckboard, movements turning steady as the small tasks took hold: rag, oil, check, reassemble. Beside him, Erich drew a nub of pencil from his pocket and a scrap of paper scissored from a ration label. He stared at it for a long time.

"Write later," Lukas said, gentle.

"I'm afraid if I wait, the words will leave," Erich murmured. He didn't write. He folded the scrap, put it away.

Matthias watched them both, mouth quirked. "I can't write poems," he said. "But I can dig. Come on."

They shuffled down to the battered sector that yesterday's shelling had chewed open. The wall slumped where it should have been sharp; water seeped in where it shouldn't be. Shovels bit the mud with dull thunks. Men worked in a rhythm older

77

than the war: lift, throw, stamp, plank, sandbag, tie. The sun climbed a hand's width and gave no warmth.

Now and then, a single crack from across the way reminded them that the other side still breathed. A bullet thudded into the parapet two feet above Lukas's head. He paused, counted to five without meaning to, then dug again. Somewhere behind them, the burial detail moved past with a stretcher and a length of canvas. No one looked up.

By midmorning, the trench held its shape again. The corporal passed, grunted, and chalked a mark on a post. "Wire party—your turn."

They traded shovels for gloves and cutters and eased toward the gap they'd forced yesterday. The wire lay snarled like a nest of iron snakes, the bodies still caught in it, stiff with cold. Erich swallowed hard and worked without letting his eyes settle. Matthias hummed under his breath, a tune that might have been a harvest song if you didn't listen too closely.

"Careful," Lukas said when Erich's sleeve snagged. He freed him, fingers quick, and for a moment Erich's hand gripped his wrist—thanks, apology, fear—then let go.

Near noon, a runner slid along the trench, panting. "Rotate! First squad, stand down. Second to carrying party—ammo to the forward sap by dusk."

"That's us," Matthias said, cheerfulness nailed in place. "Rest while you can, boys. Goose dinner in…oh, six years?"

They took their rest in the thin shade of the trench wall. Lukas leaned back, closed his eyes, and saw the boy he'd shot topple again into mud. He forced the image away with a breath, replaced it with the thought of Anna's hands cooling a fever, the warmth of a room without gun oil in the air. He opened his eyes before the picture could blur.

The medics passed, sleeves dark at the cuffs, faces pinched with tiredness. One of them paused, nodded toward Matthias's bandage. "Let me see."

"It's fine," Matthias began, but the medic had already peeled back the strips. He tsked, cleaned the edges with something that stung, wrapped it neat. "Don't be clever. Infection likes brave men best."

"Then it will have to go hungry," Matthias said, and flashed him a grin that almost reached his eyes.

Afternoon crawled. The sky clouded, and the light turned the color of pewter. A distant barrage rumbled and moved on. The runner returned, breath fogging. "Carrying party—now."

They loaded crates of rifle rounds onto a sledge and bent their shoulders to it, working up the shallow communication trench that stank of chalk and old fear. The sap was a scraped finger into open ground, barely deeper than a man's waist. They crouched, passed boxes hand to hand, and Lukas felt the old rhythm take him again: lift, pass, duck, listen. Across the flat, a machine gun stitched the air, impatient but blind.

When the last crate thumped down, the corporal tapped Lukas's shoulder. "You, Saxony, and the quiet one—back to first stand. Grab hot water if the kitchen still remembers how."

They reversed the path, slower now. By the time they reached their own bay, night was threatening again, the day spent as sparingly and as wastefully as all the others.

A cook had indeed remembered. He ladled a thin stew into their tins without ceremony. They ate sitting in a row, boots braced on the opposite wall. The stew tasted of onions and something like beef if you were generous. None of them complained.

After, Erich unfolded his scrap at last. He wrote a single line, careful and small, then stopped and stared as if the rest might come if he held still enough.

"What is it?" Lukas asked.

Erich shook his head. "Only a beginning."

Matthias nudged them both, eyelids heavy. "Wake me if the Kaiser drops by," he said, and slid down until his helmet tilted over his eyes.

Somewhere to their left, a man laughed too loudly and then fell quiet. Somewhere to their right, a chaplain murmured over a wrapped shape. Overhead, the first flare of the evening arced and faded.

"Together tomorrow," Lukas said, not sure if he meant it as a promise or a prayer.

Erich folded the scrap and tucked it away. "Together," he said.

They settled back into the trench's rough embrace, the day's work already smearing into the days before and after. Orders would come again. Reality would intrude again. But for one thin moment between them—three boys, chilled, sore, and breathing—that was enough.

CHAPTER EIGHT:
Rumors

The days grew colder again, though spring had officially come. Each morning, frost clung to the edges of the tents and the breath of the nurses rose like ghosts in the dim light. Anna rose before dawn, lighting the stove and checking her supplies by the thin glow of an oil lamp. She had grown used to the rhythm of waiting—but not the ache that came with it.

Since the last wave of evacuations, the camp had filled again. The wounded arrived daily, some still bleeding, some barely clinging to life. Each new stretcher carried not only a man, but whispers—rumors of where the front was moving, who had held the line, and who had not returned.

Lukas's unit was among those rumored to have gone forward near Ypres.

She heard the name first from a medic passing through, a young man with trembling hands and a bandage around his neck. "They were overrun in the low ground," he'd said quietly as she cleaned his wound. "Some made it out... most didn't."

Anna's hand had stilled on the cloth. "Did you see them? The 14th Infantry?"

He shook his head. "Only heard."

Heard. It was a cruel word. It left everything possible— hope and grief knotted together until she could no longer tell which she was breathing.

That night she sat outside her tent, the lamp extinguished to save fuel, her shawl drawn tight around her shoulders. The horizon glowed faintly with artillery flashes, like heat lightning that never stopped.

Every burst reminded her of the sound of Lukas's voice, low and steady, promising: *I'll find you when it's over.*

The wind carried the faint hum of distant guns. The war was crawling closer again; she could feel it in the way the ground seemed to tremble beneath her boots, in the hurried whispers of officers, in the way the sky seemed to press lower each night.

A nurse approached—Greta, her closest friend since training. Her apron was smudged, her dark hair loose from its pins. "You should sleep, Anna."

"I can't."

Greta sat beside her, sighing softly. "It's him, isn't it?"

Anna didn't answer, but the silence was enough.

"I've seen you looking toward the road every time a wagon comes," Greta continued gently. "You'll make yourself sick waiting."

Anna's eyes stayed fixed on the horizon. "I just need to know. Alive or dead. I need to *know*."

Greta placed a hand over hers. "None of us ever know. Not until the fighting stops."

"The fighting never stops," Anna whispered.

A long silence stretched between them, broken only by the faint rumble of artillery and the rustling of the canvas tents. Finally, Greta rose and went inside, leaving Anna alone with the night.

Anna reached into her apron pocket and pulled out a scrap of folded paper—the corner of a medical requisition form. On it, in the margin, she'd written his name. Just his name. *Lukas Schneider.*

She stared at it until her vision blurred, then folded it back carefully, as if the act of keeping it safe might somehow keep him safe, too.

The next morning brought new arrivals—more wounded, more chaos. Among them were men from the 14th.

Anna's pulse quickened as she moved from cot to cot, her voice calm and steady, even as her heart pounded. She asked the same quiet question of each man who could speak: "Did you serve with Lukas Schneider?"

Some shook their heads. Others didn't remember. One finally said, "The name sounds familiar. Tall fellow, gray eyes?"

"Yes," she breathed.

"I think he was with the second wave," the soldier murmured. "We lost sight of them in the fog."

"In the fog," Anna repeated softly, as though the word itself might be a clue.

That night, when the camp finally fell quiet, she sat by her small desk and began to write a letter she couldn't send.

Lukas,

The days are long without a word from you. The guns haven't stopped, and sometimes I think they never will. But I still wait. Every wagon that comes down the road, I look for your face. Every time the wind shakes the tent, I think it might

be your step outside. If you are alive—hold fast. I will be here.
— Anna

She folded the letter and placed it beside her cot, where the lantern light flickered softly over her name and his. Outside, the wind rose again, carrying with it the sound of distant thunder—the war creeping closer, one heartbeat at a time.

And still, she waited.

* * *

The next week broke like a wave of blood and mud.

Before dawn, the ambulances began arriving—lines of horse-drawn wagons and motor-   lorries grinding through the rutted road, caked with filth and the stink of cordite. The air was wet and raw, the rain coming in gusts that turned the ground to slurry. From the driver's shouts to the groans of the wounded, it was a sound that made the heart falter.

Anna was already outside when the first wagon lurched to a stop. "Quickly—inside!" she called, waving the orderlies forward. The smell hit her first—blood, smoke, and earth. One by one, they carried the stretchers into the tent, laying the men in long rows.

"Shot through the lung," murmured Greta, leaning over the first cot. "This one might not last the hour."

Anna moved to the next. The man's arm was gone from the elbow down, crudely bandaged. She pressed the gauze tighter, whispering, "You're safe now," though she barely believed it herself.

Outside, the rain drummed harder. The ground shook again—distant guns, steady and relentless. They were close enough now that each blast felt like a heartbeat beneath her feet.

"Keep the morphine to half doses," said the doctor grimly. "We're running low again."

Anna nodded. Her hands were slick with blood, her apron soaked through, but she did not stop. Hour after hour, she worked—wrapping, cutting, cleaning, whispering comfort that no one could hear above the din.

Each new stretcher that entered made her heart jolt. She found herself scanning every face, even before she had finished with the last—looking for him. Lukas. Hoping. Fearing.

By evening, the tent was full. The air was heavy with the heat of too many bodies and the metallic scent of blood. The lamps flickered, casting weary shadows on the walls.

A medic entered, wiping his brow. "They're bringing more from Ypres Ridge. Another convoy."

Anna froze, her heart clenching. "From Ypres?"

He nodded. "The 14th held the flank before it fell."

Her knees weakened. She gripped the edge of a table. "The 14th…" she repeated, her voice almost a whisper.

She wanted to ask if he'd seen Lukas, but the words wouldn't form. She only nodded and forced herself back to work.

Through the night, the wagons kept coming. She stopped counting the hours, stopped thinking altogether. Her world became the narrow space between one man's pain and the next.

At one point, she stepped outside to catch her breath. The rain had stopped. The horizon glowed faintly red with distant fires, and the smell of gunpowder carried on the wind. She pressed a trembling hand to her chest.

"Please," she whispered into the darkness. "Please let him be alive."

A soft voice behind her said, "Anna?"

It was Greta, her face pale under the lamplight. "You should sleep."

"I can't."

Greta hesitated. "They said another battalion was lost in the counterfire. We may see more in the morning. Or none at all."

Anna nodded, staring toward the horizon. "None at all," she repeated. "That's what I fear most of all."

Greta placed a hand on her shoulder. "If he's alive, he'll find you. You said he promised."

Anna turned her face away, blinking back tears. "Promises don't stop bullets."

She went back inside. The tent was quieter now—the kind of quiet that came only after the worst had passed. Many of the men were sleeping under the haze of morphine. Others had already grown still.

She moved between them, adjusting blankets, closing eyes that would not open again. And as she did, she felt the

86

hollow ache inside her deepen—grief, exhaustion, and something more fragile: the terror that hope itself was slipping away.

When at last she sank onto the stool beside her small desk, dawn was breaking. The canvas glowed faintly gold, and the first birds began to call beyond the lines.

Anna picked up her unsent letter to Lukas and read it again, tracing her name at the bottom with a bloodstained thumb. Her lips moved silently around the words she had written days ago: *If you are alive—hold fast. I will be here.*

Her hands trembled as she folded it shut. She pressed it to her chest, closed her eyes, and breathed the one truth she still had left.

"I will be here."

Outside, the wind stirred again—cold, carrying the smell of smoke and the faint, distant echo of artillery—and Anna, weary to her bones, lifted her head and waited.

CHAPTER NINE:
Heidelberg

The road to her parents 'village curved through fields that had once been gold with barley. Now the stubble lay flat beneath a thin gray mist. Anna pulled her cloak tighter as she walked, her boots crunching over frost and mud. Far off, the low rumble of guns rolled like distant thunder — constant, familiar, and wearying.

Her parents 'cottage stood where it always had, at the bend of the road where the chestnut tree leaned toward the brook. Smoke rose from the chimney, smelling of wood and coffee. For a moment, as she stepped through the gate, it was almost possible to forget the war.

Abraham Müller met her at the door, his spectacles fogged from the warmth inside. "Anna! You've come," he said softly, gathering her into an embrace that still smelled faintly of pipe tobacco and ink.

Inside, her mother, Miriam, was stirring soup on the stove. The little house felt the same — lace curtains, faded prayer books, the old clock ticking with stubborn regularity. But even here, the war had left its mark: rationed candles, blackout curtains, and a silence that lingered too long after each sentence.

"Sit, Liebchen," Miriam said. "You look thin again. You work too much."

"I can't leave them," Anna answered, slipping off her cloak. "The men... they come in faster than we can treat them."

Her mother ladled soup into bowls. "And for what?" she whispered. "More sons, more fathers sent to die. The Kaiser calls it honor. I call it madness."

Her father's hand stilled over his cup. "Careful," he murmured, but not sharply. Then, after a pause, "We do what we can. Quietly."

Anna looked up. "I know."

Miriam exchanged a glance with him before speaking. "Messages, supplies — small things. The British lines aren't so far as they say. There are people who pass through the forest at night."

Anna's spoon froze midway to her lips. "You're still helping the Allies?" she breathed.

Her father's eyes, once gentle, now held a weary conviction. "If it shortens this war by even a day, if it saves one life — Ja."

The clock ticked. The wind rattled the shutters. Anna's heart tightened, torn between pride and fear. "If they find out..."

"They won't," he said. "You mustn't speak of it, even at the hospital. Not a word, Anna."

The soup had gone cold, but none of them noticed. The little kitchen glowed in lamplight, soft and golden against the gloom outside. Wind pressed against the shutters, carrying faint echoes of distant guns — reminders that even here, peace was borrowed, not earned.

Anna sat with her hands wrapped around her cup of hot coffee, trying to gather her thoughts. Her mother watched her closely, as she always did when Anna came home from the hospital — searching her daughter's face for the things she would not say.

"You're quieter than usual," Miriam said softly. "Is it the work? Or someone you've met?"

Anna's lips curved faintly, though her eyes stayed on the cup. "There's a soldier," she admitted after a pause. "He came in a while back. His name is Lukas Schneider. From Bavaria, I think."

Her father glanced up. "Another patient?"

"Ja," she said. "But not like the others." She hesitated, then went on. "He was badly wounded — shrapnel in his thigh. I thought we would lose him that first night. But he fought... as if something in him refused to let go."

Her mother's hands stilled over the tablecloth. "And you've been tending him since."

Anna nodded. "I was. He's already been sent back to the front. He's young, barely older than I am. Polite. Quiet. But there's something steady about him. Even when he was in pain, he didn't complain. He listened." She smiled faintly, remembering. "He asked me if I missed home. I told him I was close enough to walk. He said I was lucky — that all he wanted was to see green fields again, and not trenches."

Abraham sighed, rubbing the bridge of his nose beneath his spectacles. "Anna... you must be careful. A nurse's duty is to heal, not to feel."

"I know," she said. "And yet..." She trailed off, the words trembling on the edge of something she couldn't yet name. "There's so little kindness left in the world, Papa. When you see even a flicker of it, you hold on."

Her mother reached across the table and touched her hand. "It's human to care. But the war is cruel to those who hope too much."

Anna looked at her then, seeing not reproach but fear — the same fear that haunted her every time the wagons came in. "I'm not a fool," she said gently. "I know what this war does to men. But Lukas... there's something good in him. Something I don't want the war to destroy."

Her father leaned back, studying her face, torn between worry and reluctant understanding. "Then pray for him," he said quietly. "Pray he comes through it. And pray that when this madness ends, there will still be something left worth loving."

The clock struck eight. Outside, a shell boomed in the far distance, followed by a long, shivering silence. Anna drew her cloak around her shoulders, preparing to return to the hospital before curfew. She nodded slowly, but the thought weighed on her as she kissed them goodbye. As she stepped into the cold night, her mother called softly after her: "Be careful, Anna. The war watches everything — even the heart."

Anna paused, looking back at the lamplight glowing in the window. "I know, Mama," she said. "But sometimes, the heart doesn't listen."

The smoke from their chimney trailed into a darkening sky, and the sound of guns was louder now, carried on the wind.

She walked on, her boots crunching over the frozen ground, and in the quiet between cannon fire, she found herself whispering Lukas's name.

By the time she reached the edge of the field hospital, the first wagons were already arriving — stretchers lined with the broken and the dying. The war had found her again.

CHAPTER TEN:
Tending the Wounded

The snow came early that year, fine and powdery, falling soundlessly over the shattered fields. By then, Anna had stopped counting the days. The war had become a season of its own—gray, endless, without beginning or end.

The medical tents were half-buried beneath drifts, their ropes creaking in the wind. Inside, the lamps hissed and sputtered, their light painting long, trembling shadows across the rows of cots. Anna's fingers were raw from washing, binding, and working in the cold.

But still, she listened.

Every arrival—every column of smoke on the horizon, every motor-lorry rumbling up the road—sent her heart hammering.

That morning, the sound came again: the deep, uneven rumble of engines approaching. Anna dropped the roll of gauze she'd been holding and hurried to the tent flap.

Wagons and trucks crawled toward the camp, their sides plastered with mud. Men inside were slumped against each other, hollow-eyed and silent. Some stared blankly; others cried softly under their breath.

Greta appeared at her side, wiping her hands on her apron. "Another wave from the Ridge," she murmured. "Ypres again."

Anna's throat tightened. "Do they say which units?"

Greta shook her head. "Only that the 14th is among them."

The words struck like a blow. Anna stood frozen as the first stretchers came down. The men were barely recognizable under layers of mud and blood. Some moaned softly; others lay too still.

She stepped forward, helping to lift the first stretcher. "Get them inside! Quickly!"

For hours she worked again—mechanically, tirelessly— her hands moving without thought. Yet beneath the rhythm of tending wounds, her mind whispered his name over and over.

Lukas.

At one point, she paused by a soldier whose face was half-hidden beneath grime. His eyes fluttered open as she pressed a cloth to his shoulder wound.

"You're safe," she murmured automatically.

He squinted at her, his lips pale and cracked. "Nurse…" His voice was weak, roughened by smoke and exhaustion. "Schneider… Lukas Schneider… was with us."

Anna froze. "You know him?"

He nodded faintly. "Yes, ma'am. Same trench. Ypres Ridge."

Her heart leapt and twisted all at once. "Is he alive?"

The soldier's brow furrowed as if trying to remember. "He was… last I saw. Carried the lieutenant when the line broke."

"Carried him?"

"Under fire." The man gave a faint, weary smile. "Fool thing to do. But that's Lukas. Wouldn't leave anyone."

Anna swallowed hard. "And then?"

He closed his eyes, voice barely a whisper. "The trench collapsed. I… I don't know what happened after."

Her hands trembled. "Do you mean he was buried?"

"I don't know," the soldier murmured again, slipping back into delirium. "Maybe he made it out. Maybe not."

Anna stood motionless for a long time, the cloth slipping from her fingers. Around her, the tent was alive with movement—nurses, doctors, groans, the rustle of canvas—but she heard none of it.

When Greta touched her shoulder, she flinched.

"What did he say?" Greta asked softly.

Anna's lips parted, but the words caught in her throat. "He was alive. He carried another man… and then the trench fell."

Greta's expression softened. "Then he might still be alive."

"Or buried beneath the mud," Anna whispered.

The wind outside rose, whistling through the seams of the tent. She stared at her trembling hands, still streaked with blood.

That night, she couldn't sleep. The storm had grown worse; snow beat against the canvas like a steady drum. The lanterns guttered low, and the cold crept in through every gap.

She sat by her small desk, staring at the letter she'd written him weeks ago. The ink had faded where her tears had fallen the night before. She took up her pen again and began another.

Lukas,

They say you were at Ypres. That you were seen carrying a wounded man. No one knows what became of you after that. Some say the trench collapsed. I cannot—will not—believe it.

If you are alive, please hold on. If you are lost… please forgive me for not being there.

Her hand faltered. She drew in a shaky breath and pressed the paper to her chest, whispering into the darkness, "Don't let this be the end."

Outside, the snow kept falling—soft, ceaseless, and silent—as though the heavens themselves were trying to cover the scars of the world.

And still, Anna waited.

CHAPTER ELEVEN:
Lukas

The world had become nothing but noise and smoke.

Lukas crouched behind the fractured wall of a farmhouse, the air thick with dust and the copper sting of blood. Around him, the ground trembled beneath the thunder of artillery. The battalion had been ordered to hold the line at dawn, but the dawn had come —and hell had come with it.

He pressed his hand to the leg Anna had mended. The wound had long since scabbed over, but the scar still burned, as if reminding him of the promise he had made—to return to her. *"You must come back,"* she had said softly that morning, her hands trembling as she fastened the button of his tunic. *"You must."*

A shell exploded not twenty meters away, showering him with dirt and shrapnel. Lukas ducked, heart pounding. Around him, men shouted orders, screamed for medics, prayed to any God still listening. The lieutenant was dead; the lines were folding. Lukas gritted his teeth and pushed forward, crawling through the mud toward the nearest trench.

He could barely hear his own voice over the chaos as he called to his men. "Fall back! Regroup by the ridge!" His throat was raw from smoke, his face streaked with soot. One of his comrades, Erich, stumbled beside him, clutching his shoulder. Lukas hauled him up, dragging him toward the ridge even as bullets hissed past.

"Where's Mathias?"

Erich shook his head. "I don't know."

In the blur of battle, Lukas lost all sense of time. Hours might have passed—or minutes. His body moved on instinct, every thought narrowed to survival, to the ache in his leg, to the memory of Anna's eyes when he'd left her.

Then, silence. The shelling stopped. Smoke drifted low across the cratered field, ghostlike. The air hung heavy with the moans of the wounded.

Lukas blinked, dazed, and realized he was still alive. Erich lay beside him, unconscious but breathing. Around them, the field was strewn with bodies. He crawled toward what had once been their forward line and saw the tattered flag—still there, clinging to a broken post.

He tore it free, pressing it against his chest. "For them," he whispered. And for her.

As dusk fell, Lukas led the few survivors toward what was left of the road. His leg screamed with every step, but he didn't stop—not until they reached the shadow of the trees, far from the battlefield's ruin.

When he finally collapsed beside the others, he stared up at the bruised sky and let himself breathe. For the first time since the battle began, his mind returned to Anna—her voice, her quiet strength, the way her hands had trembled when she'd bandaged him.

He had kept his promise. Barely.

But as he closed his eyes against the fading light, Lukas knew that survival was only half the battle. Getting back to her—through the wreckage, through the endless march of war—that was the other half. And he would not break that promise. Not while he still drew breath.

* * *

Anna was rinsing bandages in a tin basin when a nurse burst into the tent, face pale, voice tight.

"They've brought in survivors from the ambush near Ypres. A whole unit—torn to pieces."

Anna's hands stilled. The water dripped red into the basin, rhythmic as a clock. Ypres. She remembered the name from whispered conversations at her parents 'kitchen table. Just three nights before, her father had passed a scrap of coded notes to the man who came at dusk—a railway schedule, a list of troop placements, and, yes, the mention of a company moving east from Lille. He had said it was vital to stop them. She had not questioned.

She hurried to the ward. The wounded were carried in by the dozen, mud-caked and hollow-eyed. Groans filled the air, punctuated by the barked orders of doctors. Anna pressed forward, scanning faces.

Then she saw him.

Lukas.

He lay half-conscious on a stretcher, his uniform shredded, his arm and leg slick with blood. Shrapnel had torn across his shoulder and ribs. His lips moved, forming her name though no sound came.

Anna dropped to her knees beside him, clutching his hand. "I'm here, Lukas. You'll be all right."

But her heart roared with guilt. *This is what I have done. My family's words brought the Allies down on his head.*

As she worked—binding his wounds, cooling his fevered skin—fragments of memory cut through her mind: her father's grave voice, her mother's trembling hands, the courier's dark coat disappearing into the night. They had meant to help end the war, to save lives, to weaken the machine tearing Europe apart. They hadn't meant this.

When Lukas stirred, eyes clouded with pain, he whispered hoarsely, "They knew we were coming... it was as if they waited for us."

Anna's chest tightened. She bent her head so he would not see her tears. *If he ever learns the truth...*

* * *

The hospital quieted after the rush of the wounded, but Anna could not find rest. She sat at Lukas's bedside, watching the rise and fall of his chest. His bandages were clean now, his fever broken to a damp sheen on his brow. Relief should have flooded her. Instead, guilt gnawed at her bones.

Every time she closed her eyes, she saw her father's handwriting on that folded scrap—the timetable, the troop position, the words *east from Lille.* She heard the courier's boots fading into the night. She had carried the lamp that evening, her hand trembling as she lit the way. And now, the memory was smeared with blood.

Lukas stirred. His eyes fluttered open, hazy with exhaustion, but when they fixed on her, they warmed. His lips curved faintly. "Anna... you stayed."

Her throat closed. She smoothed the damp hair from his forehead. "Of course I stayed."

He squeezed her hand, weak but insistent. "We lost so many. Have you seen my friends? Mathias and Erich? I last saw them right before the explosion," he choked, his face crumbled, his breath hitched. "It was terrible…" He shook his head slowly. But then he looked up at her, into her eyes. "I came back. Because of you."

Tears burned behind her eyes. He didn't know. He couldn't know. If he ever discovered the truth—that she and her family had played a part in the ambush—it would destroy him, and it would destroy them.

So Anna lied. Not in words—she could not form them—but in silence. She pressed her forehead against his hand, whispering, "Rest now. You're safe."

But when she stepped outside the ward, the night air bit deep. Her mother waited near the gate, shawl drawn close, eyes hollow with the same knowledge.

"You saw him?" her mother asked softly.

Anna nodded, her voice breaking. "He lives."

Her mother reached for her hand, but Anna pulled away. "At what cost, Mama? We wanted to help. But it was his unit. His friends."

Silence stretched between them.

* * *

In the weeks that followed, Anna threw herself into her work with fiercer devotion. She bandaged wounds, changed linens, soothed fevered foreheads. For Lukas, she was steady, a quiet anchor, never wavering at his side. But inside, guilt became her shadow.

Every time Lukas smiled at her—every time he whispered her name as though it meant survival—Anna felt the wound deepen. She could not confess; the truth would shatter him. But she could not forget either.

So she bore it. Alone.

CHAPTER TWELVE:
Suspicion Falls

It was late afternoon when the officer came. His boots struck the ward floor with clipped precision, his iron-gray eyes scanning every cot as though each patient hid a secret. When they stopped on Lukas, Anna's chest clenched.

"This one," the officer said, glancing at the papers clipped to the end of the bed. "From the ambushed regiment."

Anna stepped forward. "He is recovering well. The shrapnel—"

"I'm not here for a nurse's report." His gaze cut to her, sharp as bayonet steel. "We are investigating how the Allies learned of that march. Someone is feeding them information. And this soldier's unit suffered dearly because of it."

Lukas stirred, half-conscious, but the officer's words seemed to pierce him. His hand twitched against the sheet, fingers curling. His voice rasped: "They knew… they knew we were coming."

The officer's head tilted, interest sharpening. "Ja. Exactly so. Perhaps one of the families nearby has been whispering to the enemy." His eyes narrowed, almost casually, toward Anna. "You're local, aren't you, Fräulein Müller?"

Her throat dried. "Yes… but I—my family—"

He cut her off with a thin smile. "Then you will understand why we must be thorough. Loose tongues cost German lives. We will find the source."

He left as briskly as he had come, his boots fading down the hall. Anna stood rooted, her heart hammering.

When she turned back, Lukas's eyes were open. They burned with confusion, with anger, with fear. "Your name," he whispered, weak but clear. "Müller… they think…?"

Anna's breath caught. The truth pressed against her chest, raw and unbearable. She could feel it in the silence between them: if she confessed now, he might never look at her the same again. If she lied, the guilt might crush her.

Her hands trembled as she touched his arm. "Lukas, please—rest. Don't listen to them."

But in his eyes she saw it—the seed of doubt. And she knew that sooner or later, she would have to choose: betray her family's secret, or betray Lukas's trust.

* * *

Lukas had been sitting up for two days now, his wounds bound tight, his strength returning in slow, stubborn increments. But the shadows beneath his eyes had deepened, and Anna knew it wasn't only pain that haunted him.

That evening, when the ward was quiet and the lanterns cast long pools of gold across the floor, he spoke. "Anna." His voice was low, deliberate.

She set aside the basin of water she had been carrying and turned. "Ja?"

He studied her, his gaze steady in a way that made her heart stumble. "The officer who came… he said someone betrayed us. That the Allies knew about our march." His jaw clenched, a muscle twitching. "I keep thinking of it. We walked straight into their guns as if we'd been led by the hand."

Anna's throat tightened. "Lukas—"

He leaned forward, ignoring the pain that flashed across her face, and spoke softly. "Tell me the truth. Your family—the Müllers—have they been speaking to the enemy?"

The words struck like a blow. Anna's lips parted, but no sound came. She felt the weight of every choice pressing on her chest. The memory of her father's coded notes. The courier's shadow slipping through the night. Lukas, carried half-dead into her care.

Her silence stretched too long.

Lukas's eyes darkened. "God help me, Anna, I don't want to believe it. But if it was your family… then it was you. You lit their way."

Tears welled in her eyes. She reached for his hand, but he pulled it back, trembling. "Lukas, I swear—we never meant—"

"Never meant?" His voice cracked, half-anger, half-grief. "Half my regiment is in the ground. Erich—Matthias—where are they? Are they even still alive? They bleed because someone meant well?"

Her tears spilled. "I didn't know it would be your unit," she whispered. "I thought… I thought it would help end this war sooner. I wanted to save lives. I never wanted it to touch you."

Lukas shut his eyes, head bowing. For a long moment, the only sound was his ragged breathing. Then, softer, almost broken: "And yet it did."

Anna's hands hovered, useless, aching to comfort him, but unable to bridge the gulf her secret had carved a space between them felt wider than any battlefield.

Lukas leaned forward, his face drawn and pale, anger flickering just beneath the surface.

"You knew," he said, voice low but shaking. "All this time, your parents have been helping the enemy — and you said nothing."

Anna's throat tightened. "I couldn't, Lukas. You don't understand—"

"Don't I?" He laughed harshly, the sound bitter. "I've watched friends die for Germany. I've buried boys who still wrote letters home to mothers who believed this war could be won. And you—" He stopped, the words breaking. "You tended my wounds while your own family betrayed my comrades."

Her eyes filled with tears, but she stood firm. "They aren't betraying anyone. They're trying to save lives, Lukas — all lives. You've seen what this war is. It's not victory anymore; it's slaughter."

"Betrayal is exactly what it is," he cut in, his voice rising. He gripped his crutch, knuckles white. "You're telling me your family aids the enemy while I'm bleeding for this country?"

Anna stepped closer. "You've seen what this war does. You've buried friends — we both have. My parents only want to end it sooner, to stop—"

"Stop?" He gave a bitter laugh. "Do you think it stops because your father passes a message? Because your mother whispers to some British spy? It's treason, Anna!"

She flinched as if struck. "They're good people. They want peace, Lukas. So do I."

"Peace?" he repeated, shaking his head. "There's no peace in lies. No peace in turning against your own."

His voice cracked on the last word, and for a moment the soldier fell away — just a young man too tired to bear another wound. But when she reached for him, he stepped back.

"Did you know, all this time?"

Her throat tightened. "I… I suspected. I didn't want to tell you until—"

"Until I loved you enough to forgive it?" His laugh was short and broken. "You should have told me from the start. You should have trusted me."

"I was afraid," she whispered. "You're a soldier. I thought you'd turn me in."

That hit him harder than any bullet. His hand trembled as he ran it through his hair. "After everything — after you sat by my bed, after you saved my life — you thought I would betray you?"

Tears stung her eyes. "You wouldn't have meant to. But you still could have."

He stared at her for a long time, the lamplight flickering between them like a trembling boundary neither dared cross.

"You're right about one thing," he said at last, his voice low. "I wouldn't have meant to." He reached for his coat, wincing as he pulled it on.

She moved toward him, desperate now. "Lukas, please—"

But he only shook his head. "I trusted you, Anna. I thought, in this cursed place, I'd found something honest." His voice broke, quieter now. "I was wrong."

The silence stretched between them — long, raw, and final. When she reached for his arm, he flinched back.

"Don't," he said quietly. "I trusted you, Anna. I thought... I thought you were different."

He took up his crutch, turned toward the tent flap. For a heartbeat, he paused — as if part of him longed to look back. Then he stepped out into the cold, disappearing into the darkness.

Anna stood there, breath trembling. The smell of antiseptic filled her lungs, sharp and bitter. Somewhere outside, a shell exploded — the earth shaking, the sky echoing with thunder. She pressed a hand to her chest, feeling the ache of what she could not mend. For the first time since the war began, she felt truly alone.

Inside the tent, she would still change his dressings, still steady her hands, but the air between them would be sharp with unspoken grief.

* * *

Morning crept gray and thin over the camp, cold fog curling low across the fields. Inside the hospital tents, lamps guttered out one by one as nurses moved wearily from cot to cot, changing bandages, emptying basins, whispering to men whose breath came in gasps.

Anna worked in silence. The rhythm of care was the only thing that kept her upright — clean, bind, comfort, move on. But every time she passed the far end of the tent, her heart tightened. Lukas sat there now, apart from the others, his crutch propped at his side, his face turned toward the wall.

He no longer met her eyes.

When she came near, he looked away. If another nurse offered water or checked his leg, he accepted with a polite nod. But when Anna's hand so much as brushed the edge of his cot, he tensed — a small, instinctive withdrawal that hurt more than any words could.

"Corporal Schneider?" she said softly one afternoon, forcing her voice steady. "You need the bandages changed again."

He didn't look up. "Sister Greta can do it."

Her throat closed. "She's tending the fever ward. I'll be quick."

He said nothing. The silence stretched. Finally, he shifted, letting her work, but he stared through her as if she were air.

Anna's fingers worked mechanically, unwrapping the linen, cleaning the wounds, pretending her hands didn't tremble. She felt the heat of his skin, the thrum of life beneath her touch — the same life she'd once fought to save with all her strength.

When she tied the last knot and stepped back, he said quietly, "Thank you, Sister." Not Anna. Never Anna.

She bowed her head and left before he could see her tears.

The days blurred together — the unending rhythm of blood and smoke, of screams carried on the wind. She told herself she would stop looking for him, but her eyes betrayed her at every turn. Sometimes she caught glimpses of him at the edge of the mess line, shoulders hunched, eyes shadowed, as though a weight he couldn't name had settled over him.

At night, when the shelling began again, she lay awake listening to the distant booms and wondered if he heard them too — if his thoughts ever strayed to her as hers did to him.

CHAPTER THIRTEEN:
Love Amid the Divide

Then, one afternoon, the war found them again.

It started with a distant whine — the sound every soldier and nurse learned to fear. A shell whistled overhead and struck the far slope beyond the tents, shaking the ground beneath their feet. A second followed, closer. The sky erupted in fire and dirt.

"Get down!" someone shouted.

Anna dropped behind a supply crate as canvas tore and men screamed. Another explosion sent shrapnel ripping through the side of the hospital tent, scattering cots and tables. Smoke and dust filled the air.

When the first lull came, she heard a familiar voice — hoarse, calling out from the chaos.

"Help! This way — there are wounded here!"

Lukas.

Anna rose without thinking, clutching her medical satchel, her heart pounding. She found him near the collapsed corner of the surgical tent, dragging a wounded orderly out from under a fallen beam. His face was streaked with soot, his uniform torn.

"Lukas!" she cried, rushing to him.

He looked up, startled — and in that instant, something broke through the wall between them.

"Get clear!" he shouted, pointing behind her. She turned just as another shell struck nearby, the blast hurling her forward. She hit the ground hard, breath knocked from her lungs.

Lukas was there in an instant, his arm around her shoulders, dragging her toward cover behind the supply wagon. The air smelled of gunpowder and burning canvas.

"You're bleeding," he said, his voice fierce.

"It's nothing," she gasped, trying to rise. "We have to get the others out."

He tightened his grip. "You're not going anywhere until I know you are all right."

Their eyes met — dust and fear between them, but something else too. The anger that had burned in him had cracked open into something rawer, desperate.

Another explosion rolled through the fields, but she hardly heard it.

"Why did you come for me?" she whispered.

His jaw tightened. "Because I couldn't let you die."

The smoke swirled around them, red and gray. Somewhere beyond the haze, shouts rose — men calling for help, the sound of boots and chaos. But for a heartbeat, there was only the two of them, crouched in the wreckage, the distance between them bridged by instinct stronger than pride.

Then Lukas helped her to her feet, and together they ran toward the cries of the wounded.

* * *

Darkness came early that night, thick and choking with smoke. The hospital grounds were unrecognizable — tents torn open like paper, cots splintered, instruments scattered in the mud. The shelling had stopped, but the cries had not.

Anna moved through the wreckage with a lantern in one hand and her satchel in the other, her skirt heavy with dirt and blood. Her ears rang from the blast; every sound came muffled, as though the world had been wrapped in cotton.

Lukas was beside her. He limped, dragging his bad leg through the churned mud, his sleeve torn, one arm already bandaged where a splinter had cut him. He didn't seem to notice the pain. Every time a moan rose from the darkness, he was there — steadying a fallen beam, lifting a man's shoulders, or bracing a stretcher while Anna worked.

They hardly spoke. The rhythm of survival left no room for words.

"Hold this," she said once, pressing his hands against a soldier's wound while she tied off a strip of linen. Their fingers brushed, slick with blood. Neither looked up, but the contact sent a tremor through her all the same.

Hours blurred together. Smoke burned her throat; her hands shook from fatigue. At some point, the oil in the lantern began to wane, and Lukas disappeared for a moment. She thought he'd gone — until he returned, carrying a replacement lamp and a blanket from the supply cart.

"You're freezing," he muttered, draping it over her shoulders.

She blinked at him, too tired to answer. His face was grimy, the lines of it sharper in the shifting light, but the anger she'd seen before had softened. What remained was something quieter — guilt, maybe, or the raw awareness of how easily they could have both died.

They moved on, tending to the wounded who could still be saved. When at last the cries began to fade and the fires burned low, Anna sank onto an overturned crate, her hands shaking uncontrollably. Lukas lowered himself beside her, wincing as his leg protested.

For a long time, neither spoke. Only the wind filled the silence, carrying the smell of gunpowder and smoke.

At last, Lukas said quietly, "When the shell hit… I thought you were gone."

Anna turned her head. "You came for me."

He looked at her then — truly looked — and she saw something flicker behind his eyes. "I didn't think. I just ran."

Her throat tightened. "You still hate me?"

His gaze dropped to his hands, scarred and trembling. "I don't know what I feel," he said softly. "Everything I thought I understood about loyalty, about right and wrong — it's slipping away. I was angry, yes. Maybe I still am. But when I saw you fall…" He exhaled. "There wasn't any anger left. Only fear."

Anna's eyes stung. "I never wanted to hurt you. I just wanted to keep my family safe. And you."

He gave a hollow laugh. "I don't deserve that kind of grace, Anna."

"You do," she said simply.

Silence stretched again — softer now, no longer sharp. Lukas shifted closer, his shoulder brushing hers. The lantern light danced across their faces, catching the fine tremor of exhaustion in his jaw, the soot clinging to her hair.

Finally, he said, almost to himself, "You're braver than anyone I've ever known."

"And you," she whispered, "are kinder than you think."

He looked at her for a long moment — the noise of the camp fading until there was only the sound of their breathing. Then, quietly, he said, "We'll start again. If you'll still have me."

Anna's heart ached at the words — not triumph, but fragile relief. "I never stopped."

He reached out then, hesitating just before his fingers found hers. Their hands rested together on the crate — nothing more than that — yet it felt like a vow.

Outside, the first pale light of dawn began to bleed through the smoke. Around them, the wounded still stirred and groaned, and the war pressed on. But for that one exhausted, trembling moment, there was peace between them again.

CHAPTER FOURTEEN:
The Morning After

A thin winter dawn crept over the camp, cold and colorless. Smoke still drifted above the cratered field, and the scent of burned canvas and iodine clung to everything. Nurses moved like ghosts through the rows of the wounded, whispering to one another in voices scraped raw by fatigue.

Anna's hands were still shaking as she washed them in a basin of cold water. Blood had dried beneath her nails; her sleeves were stiff with it. The night had blurred into one endless moment of fire and fear, and now there was only the fragile quiet that came after.

Lukas stood near the tent flap, leaning on his crutch. He looked worn and pale, but alive. Their eyes met briefly — a glance full of things neither dared to speak aloud.

Then came the sound of boots.

A squad of officers approached, the insignia on their collars still clean despite the wreckage around them. The lead inspector — a tall man with a hard face and the clipped voice of command — surveyed the devastation with disdain.

"Who's in charge here?"

Sister Greta stepped forward. "I am, sir. We took heavy fire from the enemy line last night. Several tents were destroyed. We did what we could."

The officer nodded curtly, then turned to the soldiers behind him. "Search the grounds. Make a full report. Command wants to know why the enemy shelling reached this far behind the line."

Anna froze where she stood. She knew what such an inspection meant: every name checked, every tent searched, every message or paper examined. The war had made suspicion a constant companion.

Lukas shifted, watching the officers fan out. "They'll question everyone," he murmured under his breath. "If anyone's been moving information, they'll look for proof."

Her throat tightened. "There isn't any. Not here. My parents—"

He silenced her with a small gesture. "Don't say it."

Two inspectors entered the tent, clipboards in hand. One of them nodded toward Anna. "You, nurse. Step forward. Your identification."

Anna reached into her apron pocket, hands trembling only slightly. "Nurse Anna Müller, Station Twelve."

The officer glanced at her card, then up at her face. "Müller?" he said slowly. "There's a Müller family near the river mill, yes?"

She felt her pulse stumble. "Yes, sir. My parents live there."

He studied her for a moment, then scribbled something on his sheet. "There have been reports of suspicious activity in that region. You'll remain available for questioning."

Lukas took a small step forward before he could stop himself. "She's been here all night, sir," he said sharply. "She pulled half the men in this tent out from under falling beams. If there's suspicion to throw around, you're looking in the wrong place."

The officer frowned. "And you are?"

"Corporal Lukas Schneider, 104th Infantry."

The man eyed him a moment longer, then nodded stiffly. "Your injuries should have you confined to recovery, Corporal. Leave the investigation to us."

Lukas said nothing more, but his jaw clenched. The inspectors moved on, their boots crunching in the mud outside.

When they were gone, Anna let out a breath she hadn't realized she was holding. Lukas turned to her, his expression tight with worry.

"They'll come back," he said quietly. "They'll ask questions — maybe even go to your parents 'home."

Anna's hands found the edge of a cot to steady herself. "Then it's already too late."

"No," he said. His voice was firm now, the soldier's steel returning. "You saved lives last night, Anna. If they look here, they'll see that. And if they look for your family—" He stopped, searching her face. "You'll tell them you know nothing."

Her eyes filled. "And you? If they ask about me?"

He hesitated. For a heartbeat, the weight of duty and affection warred in his eyes. Then he said softly, "I'll tell them the truth that matters. That you're the reason half this camp is still breathing."

Something loosened in her chest at his words — relief mixed with fear, gratitude tangled with the ache of what still hung between them.

Outside, the inspectors 'voices faded toward the next tent. Anna and Lukas stood together in the pale morning light, the silence between them no longer bitter, only fragile — a quiet truce amid the wreckage.

Anna reached for the bandage roll on the table. "You should sit," she said, her voice trembling just slightly. "Your wound will open again."

He gave a faint, weary smile. "Only if you refuse to stitch it."

For the first time in days, she almost laughed.

And as the camp stirred back to life around them — the endless machinery of war grinding on — a small, steady warmth settled between them, like the first ember of trust catching light again.

By late afternoon, the fragile calm of the morning had curdled into dread. A wind rose off the fields, cold and sharp, tugging at the torn canvas and carrying the smell of wet ash. The soldiers were still repairing the tents when the inspectors returned, their boots deliberate, their voices clipped. The entire camp seemed to shrink from their approach.

Anna was rinsing instruments when she heard her name.

"Nurse Müller."

She turned. The lead inspector stood in the doorway of the supply tent, a folded paper in his hand. Behind him, two subordinates watched her with the flat stare of men who had already made up their minds.

Her stomach turned to ice. "Yes, sir?"

"You said your parents live near the mill road?"

"Ja."

He opened the paper, careful not to smudge the wet ink. "Our patrol intercepted a runner outside the village last night. He was carrying messages sewn into the lining of his coat — correspondence written in a woman's hand. This one," he lifted the sheet slightly, "was signed *Miriam Müller*."

The tent seemed to tilt around her. The basin clattered against the floor, water spilling across the dirt.

"Do you deny that this is your mother?"

Anna's mouth went dry. "— I don't know. Let me see."

The officer handed it to her. The handwriting leapt from the page: the familiar slant of her mother's *M*, the neat, careful loops. *'Tell them the stores will be ready by the next moonless night. The Red Cross wagons will pass unhindered.'*

Her vision blurred. The paper shook in her hands.

"We've already sent word to headquarters," the inspector continued. "If your family is involved in espionage, the matter will be dealt with accordingly. Until then, you are confined to the hospital grounds."

She could barely breathe. "Sir, my mother— she's not a spy. She wants to help the wounded, that's all."

"The Allies are the wounded in question," he snapped. "We'll know the truth soon enough."

Lukas had entered halfway through, drawn by the sound of voices. He stood now in the shadow near the doorway, his face pale but composed. When the inspector turned to leave, Lukas stepped forward.

"Sir," he said evenly, "Nurse Müller was here during the attack. She hasn't left camp for days. Whatever her parents have done, it isn't her doing."

The officer studied him coldly. "You speak with certainty, Corporal Schneider. Why?"

Lukas's jaw tightened. "Because I was with her. She saved half this camp when the shells fell. She's loyal to her duty."

A pause. Then the inspector folded the letter again. "We shall see." He nodded to his men, and they left. The flap dropped behind them, cutting off the light.

The silence that followed was unbearable.

Anna sat slowly on the nearest cot, the letter still in her hands. "It's her handwriting," she whispered. "She really did it."

Lukas leaned on his crutch, watching her. "Then she meant it to do good, not harm."

"They won't see it that way when they come for her." Tears slid down her cheeks before she could stop them. "They'll arrest her, maybe my father too. And if they think I knew—"

He crouched beside her, his movement slow from pain but steady. "You didn't know. You said nothing. Let them search. Let them question. You tell the truth, nothing more."

She shook her head. "The truth doesn't save anyone anymore, Lukas."

He hesitated, then reached for the paper, folding it carefully, pressing it into her palm. "Then we find a way to save her ourselves."

Anna looked up at him, startled. "You'd help me?"

His eyes held hers — weary, conflicted, but resolute. "I can't undo what's already begun. But I can keep them from taking you with her."

Outside, the sun was sinking, bleeding into a sky the color of ash. The inspectors 'figures moved toward their horses, the letter packet sealed for transport. Somewhere beyond the hills, the guns were waking again.

Lukas straightened, his hand lingering briefly on her shoulder.

"When night falls," he said quietly, "we'll see what can be done."

* * *

By dusk, a bitter wind swept through the camp, tearing at the canvas and stinging the skin with sleet. The inspectors ' horses had left deep ruts in the mud, and word spread that their courier would ride for headquarters before dawn. Once that letter reached the regional command, there would be no chance to protect her parents.

Anna sat on a crate behind the triage tent, the lamplight catching the smears of iodine still on her hands. Every sound— the creak of the wagons, the faint metallic rhythm of sentries walking their rounds—seemed louder than it should. Lukas limped out of the shadows, wrapped in his greatcoat, the collar turned up against the wind.

"They've sealed the dispatch bag," he said. "It's in the supply shed by the telegraph station. The courier leaves at first light."

She looked up at him, her breath clouding. "You shouldn't be walking on that leg."

"And you shouldn't be planning to break military law," he answered quietly. "But here we are."

They waited until the camp settled into uneasy silence—nurses resting where they could, the guards huddled near their fires. The moon stayed hidden behind a thick veil of cloud. Lukas handed her a small lantern, its glass smoked black to dull the light.

"We go along the drainage ditch," he murmured. "No one uses it since the rain. When we reach the shed, I'll watch the road. You find the letter and burn it."

Anna nodded. Her hands trembled as she tied her cloak. "If they catch us—"

"They won't," he said, and though his voice was calm, she saw the tightness in his jaw.

They slipped into the night. The mud sucked at their boots, the air sharp with smoke and frost. Now and then, a flare rose far off along the front, bathing the horizon in brief, ghastly light. By the time they reached the edge of the supply yard, Anna's heart hammered so loudly she feared it would give them away.

The shed loomed ahead—a squat shape against the pale sky, a single lamp burning near its door. A sentry paced the fence, his rifle slung loosely over his shoulder.

Lukas touched her arm, motioning her down behind a stack of crates. They waited until the sentry stopped to light a cigarette, the match flaring briefly, then dying. In that moment of darkness, Lukas moved. He slipped behind the man, swift despite his limp, and brought the butt of his crutch down across the soldier's back. The sentry collapsed without a sound.

Anna stared, breath caught in her throat. Lukas looked back, eyes hard. "Go."

She ran low to the door. The lock was a simple latch. Inside, the shed smelled of damp rope and oiled leather. Crates lined the walls, and on the desk near the telegraph, she saw it: the inspector's dispatch bag, the red wax seal glinting faintly in the lamplight.

Her hands shook as she pulled her small knife from her apron pocket. The wax cracked under the blade with a soft snap. Inside were reports, requisition lists—and at the bottom, her mother's letter.

The sight of it made her knees go weak. For a heartbeat she just stared, remembering her mother's voice, the smell of coffee and woodsmoke. Then she struck a match.

The paper curled almost instantly, ink blackening, the flames whispering like breath. She dropped the remains into the coal stove, watching until they were ash. When the last ember died, she closed the dispatch bag and resealed it with a blob of melted wax from the lantern's rim.

Outside, Lukas hissed a warning. "Someone's coming."

She snuffed the lamp, heart racing, and slipped out just as two officers appeared at the far end of the yard. Lukas grabbed her wrist and pulled her into the ditch behind the shed. They crouched there, pressed close, the mud cold against their knees. Voices drifted past—guards complaining about the cold, boots crunching, the clink of a rifle strap.

When the sound faded, Anna let out a shaky breath. Lukas's arm was still around her, his coat brushing her cheek. She could feel the tremor running through him from pain and fear and something deeper.

"It's done," she whispered. "It's gone."

He nodded once. "Then we go before anyone finds the sentry."

They moved quickly back along the ditch, slipping through the shadows until the flicker of campfires reappeared ahead. Behind them, the clouds began to break, and a thin strip of moonlight touched the ground, revealing the churned earth where they'd been.

By the time they reached the tents, Anna's legs were shaking. She stopped at the threshold of the hospital, looking back toward the black horizon.

"They'll know someone tampered with it," she said.

"Maybe," Lukas answered. "But they won't know who."

He turned to her then, his face lined with exhaustion but his eyes steady. "You should sleep. Tomorrow, act as if nothing happened."

Anna hesitated, then reached out, catching his sleeve. "Lukas—danka."

He looked at her hand on his arm, then up at her face. "You don't owe me thanks," he said softly. "You owe me a reason to believe this was worth it."

Her answer came barely above a whisper. "I'll give you one."

CHAPTER FIFTEEN:
The Morning Discovery

A brittle frost glazed the camp by dawn. Smoke rose thin from the cook fires, mixing with the pale light that crept over the horizon. For a few fleeting minutes, the world looked almost peaceful — the ruins of the hospital tents hushed under a crust of white, the sky soft and pink.

Then the shouting began.

Anna froze where she stood by the water barrel, her hands half-submerged in icy water. Across the yard, two soldiers were running toward the telegraph shed, voices sharp with alarm. Within moments, the stillness shattered — officers barking orders, boots pounding through the mud.

Lukas appeared beside her, his expression grim. "They've found it," he said quietly. "The dispatch bag."

Her heart lurched. "What do they know?"

"Only that the seal's been tampered with. The letter's gone."

The inspector's voice cut through the air like a blade. "Search every tent. No one leaves this camp until we find who's responsible!"

Anna dried her hands quickly, forcing herself to move. "If they search the nurses 'quarters—"

Lukas's eyes flicked toward the shed, then back to her. "We didn't leave anything behind. Stay calm. Keep to your work."

He started toward the triage tent, but she caught his sleeve. "And you?"

"I'll do what soldiers do best," he said with a hollow smile. "Look like I know nothing."

By mid-morning, the camp was a storm of suspicion. Trunks overturned, supply chests pried open, men questioned one by one. The inspector strode through the chaos, eyes cold and calculating.

"The wax was broken. Someone entered the shed between midnight and two. The sentry was found unconscious — no memory of who struck him. Whoever it was had help."

Anna kept her head down, folding bandages, her pulse drumming so hard she could barely hear. The smell of iodine clung to her sleeves, and every sound seemed amplified — the scrape of boots, the rustle of papers, the faint hiss of the lamp.

When the inspector's shadow fell across her table, she froze.

"Nurse Müller."

Her heart stumbled. "Yes, sir?"

"You were confined to camp yesterday."

"Ja."

"Did you leave your quarters after lights out?"

She met his gaze. "No, sir."

A long pause. He studied her face with unnerving calm, as though searching for the smallest crack. "Strange, then," he said finally, "that your name keeps appearing wherever trouble follows. Perhaps a coincidence. Perhaps not."

He turned away, leaving the words to hang in the air like smoke.

Across the tent, Lukas watched, silent but tense. When the inspector moved on, he crossed to her side, speaking low enough that only she could hear.

"They're narrowing it down. If the sentry remembers anything — the sound of my crutch, even — it could lead to us."

Anna's hands trembled as she wrapped a fresh bandage. "What do we do?"

"Wait," he said. "And pray that the truth stays buried."

By evening, the sun dipped low, staining the sky with fire. The inspectors gathered near the telegraph shed, voices curt. Word spread quickly — the courier would still ride to headquarters, with a report of sabotage and a list of suspects.

Anna stood in the doorway of the hospital tent, exhaustion and fear washing over her. Lukas approached slowly, his limp more pronounced from the long day.

"They'll move on tomorrow," he said. "But they'll keep your name on their list."

She looked up at him, eyes hollow. "Then it's not over."

"No," he admitted. "But you're still here. That's something."

The wind picked up, carrying the clang of metal from the repair yard. The camp felt colder than before — the kind of cold that lived beneath the skin.

Anna pulled her cloak tighter, staring at the distant outline of the telegraph pole against the sunset. Somewhere out there, another war waited, quieter but no less dangerous: the war of secrets and silence.

Beside her, Lukas said quietly, "Whatever comes, we face it together now."

She turned toward him, the last light of day catching on his face — the weariness, the resolve, the fragile trust that had begun to rebuild.

And though the fear lingered, Anna felt something steadier take root beneath it — a fragile thread of courage binding them both to the uncertain dawn ahead.

* * *

The wind had turned bitter by the time the sun fell. The camp lamps flickered against the canvas walls, and from the trenches beyond came the steady, low thunder of guns — distant, but never far enough away. Inside the hospital tent, the last of the wounded slept fitfully, their breathing a ragged counterpoint to the storm outside.

Anna sat at the edge of a cot, her hands still and cold. A nurse from the next ward had slipped her a scrap of paper an hour ago, smudged and folded tight. The message was brief, written in hurried script:

"The Müllers taken near the mill road. Questioned by command. No release ordered."

Her vision had blurred the moment she read it. Now the paper lay in her lap, damp where her fingers had clutched it too long. The words seemed to burn through her palms.

Lukas entered quietly, his shadow stretching long across the canvas. He'd been out helping repair the fence line; his coat was wet with sleet, his limp more pronounced. One look at her face stopped him cold.

"What is it?"

She held out the note. He took it, eyes moving across the brief message. His jaw tightened. "When?"

"Yesterday," she whispered. "They must have gone to the house after finding the letter missing. They've arrested them both."

The silence that followed was deep, heavy with the crackle of the storm. Lukas looked down at the paper again, then slowly folded it, his fingers shaking.

"Anna… if they question them long enough—"

"I know," she said, her voice breaking. "If they think I had anything to do with it, they'll come for me next."

He crouched beside her cot, lowering his voice to a rough whisper. "Then we can't wait for them to decide. We go tonight."

She stared at him. "Go? Where?"

"South, toward the woods beyond the rail line. There's a village there, mostly empty. Refugees pass through. We can disappear until this blows over."

She shook her head, tears glinting. "Lukas, if we run, it proves everything. They'll say I was guilty. That my parents were spies and I was their accomplice."

"If you stay, they'll hang that guilt on you anyway," he said. "Do you think Command cares about proof? They just need someone to punish."

The rain lashed against the tent, sudden and wild. Anna rose to her feet, pacing the narrow aisle between the cots. "And what about you? You'd be deserting. They'll shoot you if they find you."

He managed a faint, humorless smile. "They nearly did once already. What's one more risk?"

She stopped, turning toward him. "You'd really do that — for me?"

He met her gaze, the faint lamplight catching the line of his face, the exhaustion in his eyes. "For you, ja. And because I'm done fighting for something that's turned men into ghosts."

The tent fell quiet except for the wind and the far-off echo of guns. Anna pressed her hands to her temples, torn between fear and the fierce, aching pull of hope.

"My parents," she whispered. "If we leave, we abandon them."

Lukas stood, wincing slightly as his bad leg took his weight. "You can't save them if you're in chains, Anna. But if we can reach the Allied line — or even neutral ground — we might find a way to get word to them, to trade names for safety."

She hesitated. The idea sounded impossible, reckless — yet it burned bright in the darkness, the only thing that didn't feel like despair.

Finally, she nodded. "Then we leave before dawn."

Lukas exhaled, relief flickering briefly across his face. "Pack only what you need. Food, water, your medical kit."

She turned to the cabinet, gathering what she could with trembling hands. The steady rhythm of her work steadied her heart.

Outside, thunder rolled again, closer now. Lukas reached for his crutch and limped toward the entrance, glancing back at her one last time.

"It's a long road ahead," he said softly. "But at least it's ours to choose."

Anna paused, clutching the strap of her satchel. "Then let's choose it together."

The lantern flame swayed as the wind tore through the tent. Beyond the camp, the black shape of the forest waited, vast and uncertain — but somewhere past that darkness lay the fragile promise of freedom.

CHAPTER SIXTEEN:
The Escape

The storm broke just after midnight. Wind tore across the camp, rattling the tin roofs and twisting the guy ropes of the tents until they screamed. Rain fell in sheets, driving sideways through the open ground. For once, it drowned out even the guns.

Anna waited in the dim light of the dispensary, the small satchel slung across her shoulder. Inside it were bandages, morphine, a flask of water, and the photograph of her parents she had carried since her first day at the front. Each second stretched thin as a wire.

Then the flap opened, and Lukas slipped inside, soaked and pale beneath his hooded coat. His crutch was wrapped in cloth to muffle the sound.

"The north sentry took shelter by the boiler house," he said, his voice barely a whisper. "We have one chance."

Anna nodded, drawing her cloak tight. Lightning flashed through the slit in the canvas, throwing their shadows across the walls like fleeing ghosts.

They stepped out into the rain.

The ground had turned to a river of mud, sucking at their boots with every step. The campfires had been smothered by the downpour, leaving only the occasional lantern glowing faintly through the sheets of water. Thunder rolled overhead, covering their movements.

They moved between the tents, staying low, avoiding the glow of light and the scattered silhouettes of the guards. Once, Anna stumbled on a coil of wire; Lukas caught her arm just before she fell. His grip was firm, steadying, the same touch that had once anchored her in the worst nights of the hospital.

"Easy," he murmured. "Follow me."

They skirted the perimeter fence, where the barbed wire sagged under the weight of the rain. The ditch beyond it was half-flooded. Lukas knelt, cutting a gap in the wire with the small pair of pliers he'd stolen from the mechanics 'tent. The metal snapped with a muted *ping*.

"Go," he said. "I'll follow."

Anna slipped through, her cloak snagging on a barb. She tore it free, feeling the fabric rip, then crawled up the far bank. The forest loomed ahead — a wall of darkness, the trees thrashing in the wind. Behind her, Lukas dragged himself through the gap, breathing hard.

They paused in the shelter of the trees, chests heaving. For the first time, the sounds of the camp were muffled, swallowed by the storm.

"We did it," she whispered.

"Not yet," Lukas answered. He pointed toward the faint glow of lanterns moving near the supply yard. "If they do a patrol, they'll see the cut wire."

As if summoned by his words, a voice shouted in the distance, followed by the sharp beam of a searchlight sweeping the field. Anna caught the glint of bayonets.

"Run," Lukas said.

They plunged deeper into the woods. Branches whipped at their faces; the ground was slick with leaves and roots. The light flashed behind them, voices rising above the wind.

Lukas's limp slowed them, but he pressed on, jaw clenched, refusing to let her outpace him.

A shot cracked — distant, but close enough to make Anna's heart leap. They ducked behind a fallen tree as the beam passed overhead, slicing through the rain like a blade. Lukas gripped her hand, his breath ragged.

"Keep going east," he whispered. "There's a ravine ahead. If we reach it, they'll lose our trail."

She nodded, and they moved again, half-running, half-sliding through the mud. The forest thickened, the storm muting the world into gray. The shouting grew fainter, swallowed by the rain.

At last, they reached the ravine — a narrow, rocky descent choked with water. Lukas helped her down first, then followed, wincing with every movement. They crouched beneath an overhang, the roar of the storm filling the hollow like a living thing.

Anna leaned against the cold stone, trembling. Lukas sank down beside her, pressing a hand to his leg. Blood seeped through his bandage, washed thin by the rain.

"You're bleeding," she whispered.

"It's nothing," he said, though his voice was tight. "We're out. That's what matters."

She turned to him, rain streaming down her face. For a long moment, they just sat there — soaked, shaking, alive. Then, slowly, she reached for his hand. He hesitated only a second before his fingers closed around hers.

"We'll find them," she said softly. "My parents. Somehow."

He looked at her — tired, determined, the glimmer of something still unbroken in his eyes. "We will. But for tonight…" He glanced toward the forest above them, the storm still raging. "We survive."

Lightning flashed again, lighting the hollow in stark white. In that instant, Anna saw them as they were — two fugitives bound by love and loss, the war at their backs and an uncertain world ahead.

The thunder rolled, long and low, as they pressed closer beneath the rock and waited for the night to pass.

* * *

By dawn, the storm had thinned to a whisper. The rain no longer fell in torrents but in fine, steady threads that hung in the air like breath. The forest steamed faintly under the pale light, every branch dripping, every leaf glistening as though newly forged from glass.

Anna woke first. Her cloak was soaked, her fingers numb, her body aching from cold and exhaustion. Beside her, Lukas slept in a shallow doze, his crutch propped against the rock. The bandage on his leg was dark with fresh blood. She touched his arm gently.

"Lukas," she whispered. "It's morning."

He stirred, opening his eyes to the gray light. For a moment, he seemed disoriented, then the memory of the night returned, and his jaw tightened. "Are they following?"

She listened — only the sound of dripping water, a raven's croak far off. "No voices. No dogs."

He sat up slowly, grimacing. "Then we move before they start searching again."

Anna opened her satchel, fingers stiff as she unwrapped a clean strip of linen. "Let me see your leg."

"We don't have time."

"We'll make time."

Her tone left no room for argument. She peeled back the wet bandage, cleaned the wound with what little alcohol remained, and tied the fresh linen snugly. He said nothing through the pain, only clenched his jaw until she finished. When she looked up, she saw gratitude flicker in his eyes — quiet, wordless, and deeper than speech.

They climbed from the ravine into a forest washed clean by rain. The air smelled of pine and damp earth. Mist hung low between the trees, curling around their ankles as they walked. Every sound seemed enormous — the snap of a twig, the distant drip of water from the branches — as though the world itself held its breath for them.

After an hour, they reached a clearing where the trees thinned and the sky showed faint color. The east glowed with a fragile strip of gold, the first true light they had seen in days. Anna stopped, her breath catching.

"It's beautiful," she said softly.

Lukas followed her gaze. "It almost doesn't look real."

They stood there a moment, the light spilling over them, warming their faces. Then Lukas's expression hardened again.

"We can't take the road. Too open. We'll keep to the woods until night. There's a river not far from here — maybe a bridge, or a crossing."

Anna nodded, tightening her cloak. "And then?"

"Then we see who still believes in mercy."

They walked until the mist began to burn away. Birds stirred in the canopy, shaking rain from their wings. Once, they heard the low growl of an engine far off — trucks or patrol cars — and froze, pressed against the wet bark until the sound faded.

By midday, they found the river — wide, gray, swollen from the storm. The current was fierce, foaming around broken stones. A half-collapsed bridge jutted from one bank like a shattered rib.

Lukas leaned on his crutch, studying it. "We can't cross there."

Anna pointed upstream. "The water's narrower that way. We might wade across if we find a shallow bend."

"You'll freeze."

"We'll freeze if we stay."

He gave a short nod, conceding. "We follow the river, then."

They moved along the bank, boots sinking into the mud, the roar of the water constant in their ears. After a while, Anna glanced sideways at him.

"Do you ever think," she asked quietly, "that we'll see home again?"

He didn't answer at first. Then, softly: "I don't know if the world we left still exists. But if it doesn't, we'll build another."

Something in his tone — steady, defiant — sent warmth through her chest despite the cold. She reached for his hand, just briefly, and he didn't pull away.

Above them, the clouds began to break at last, revealing thin streaks of blue. The forest glittered under the newborn light. Behind them lay the camp, the war, the life they'd both been meant to live. Ahead stretched only uncertainty — but it was their own, and for the first time, that felt like freedom.

They kept walking, their footprints vanishing quickly in the soft, wet earth, swallowed by the awakening day.

* * *

By late afternoon, the weak sunlight had faded again behind a curtain of low clouds. The forest darkened early, the damp air growing colder by the hour. Anna and Lukas had followed the river until their legs ached and the smell of smoke from some distant farm drifted faintly through the mist.

They stopped beneath a stand of pines to rest. Lukas leaned against a tree, his breath visible in the chill air, his crutch sunk deep in the wet soil. Anna knelt by a patch of dry leaves, opening her satchel to check their remaining supplies — half a loaf of bread, a few bandages, and her last strip of morphine.

"We'll find a barn," Lukas murmured. "A roof, maybe some warmth."

She nodded, though her eyes flicked nervously toward the river. "Do you hear that?"

At first, only the rustle of wind and dripping branches. Then — faint but unmistakable — the *clack* of boots on stone, the metallic rattle of weapons. Voices. Male. German.

Lukas straightened instantly, every muscle tensing. "Patrol."

Anna's heart lurched. "How did they—"

"They've been tracking the river. Maybe they saw our footprints."

The voices grew louder, carried by the wind — laughter, rough and unguarded. One of the men shouted something about finding shelter before nightfall. Another laughed again, closer this time.

Lukas grabbed her hand. "Come."

They slipped off the path and into the underbrush, crouching low. The ground was soft with moss, their breath steaming in the cold. The soldiers 'voices drifted nearer — the scrape of a rifle butt against a tree, the metallic click of a lighter.

Anna pressed a hand over her mouth, forcing her breath silent. Lukas crouched beside her, his arm brushing hers, the faint tremor of his exhaustion trembling through them both.

"Two more weeks of this mud and I'll lose my mind," one soldier muttered.

"Command says there's a nurse and a deserter out here," another replied. "If they're smart, they're halfway to France by now."

"Smart?" A harsh laugh. "Not if they think they can outrun the Kaiser's dogs."

Anna felt her pulse pounding in her throat. Lukas's fingers found hers in the dark, steady and firm — not to reassure, but to remind her to stay still. The searchlight beam swept the woods once, twice, slicing through the branches a few paces away. She could smell the soldiers 'tobacco, hear the jingle of a canteen.

Then — silence. A cough. A voice muttering, "Nothing here." The boots turned, crunching back toward the river. The sound faded, swallowed by the wind.

Anna stayed frozen until Lukas exhaled. "They're gone," he whispered.

She sagged against the trunk, the tension spilling out of her in a shudder. Lukas's face was pale, and beads of sweat were along his brow. His leg throbbed visibly beneath the torn cloth. She reached out, touching his arm.

"You can't walk farther tonight. You'll collapse."

"We can't stay here either. If they come back—"

"Then we hide better," she said, scanning the darkness. A flicker caught her eye — the faint outline of stone through the trees. "There. A wall."

They moved cautiously through the undergrowth until the shape emerged: the remnants of an old chapel, roof half-collapsed, its doorway choked with ivy. Inside, the air smelled of damp wood and earth, but it was dry. Anna helped Lukas lower himself against the wall, then knelt to light the small oil lamp she carried. The flame bloomed, soft and gold, painting the broken altar in shadow.

For a long time, they said nothing. The lamp flickered, casting their faces in the same warm light. Lukas leaned back, closing his eyes. "It's strange," he murmured. "Even now, with them so close… this is the first place that's felt safe in months."

Anna sat beside him, her head resting lightly against his shoulder. The chapel walls creaked in the wind. She could feel his heartbeat — slow, unsteady, but alive.

"We'll sleep a little," she whispered. "Then keep moving."

"You first," he said, voice slurred with exhaustion.

But she didn't. She listened until his breathing deepened, until the storm outside softened to a whisper and the forest seemed to exhale around them. Only then did she close her eyes, her hand still curled loosely around his.

Beyond the chapel walls, the soldiers 'voices rose faintly once more, distant this time, fading into the rain. The danger wasn't gone — it would never truly be gone — but for this single night, they were safe enough to sleep.

The light came thin and slow, seeping through the gaps in the chapel roof like spilled milk. Rain had stopped sometime in the night; now the air hung still and heavy, smelling of wet stone and pine. A pale mist drifted through the doorway, curling around the broken altar and the fallen beams.

Anna stirred first. Her cloak was damp, her back stiff from the stone floor. Lukas still slept beside her, his head tilted against the wall, breath shallow but even. For a few moments, she just watched him — the lines of fatigue softened in sleep, the faint flicker of light across his face. He looked younger this way, almost like the man he might have been before the war.

A bird called outside, low and uncertain. She rose quietly, pulling her satchel close, and pushed aside the ivy at the doorway. The forest beyond was washed clean, the trunks dark with moisture, drops of water glinting like glass in the early light.

She stepped outside, drawing a deep breath of the cold air. Somewhere nearby, water ran — a small stream trickling toward the river. The world felt new, but fragile, like something still deciding whether it wished to live again.

Behind her, Lukas's voice broke the silence. "You should have woken me."

She turned. He was sitting up now, rubbing his eyes, his hair damp from the mist.

"You needed rest," she said softly. "Your leg?"

"Still there," he muttered, testing the bandage with a grimace. "For now."

He used his crutch to push himself up, standing carefully. For a moment, he just looked around the ruin — the way the light filtered through the broken roof, the tangle of vines over the altar.

"Strange place," he said. "Half broken, half holy."

"It feels safe," she said. "But we can't stay."

He nodded. "East, I think. Toward the French line. There are villages in that direction — maybe farmers who'll take pity."

Anna hesitated. "And if they don't?"

"Then we keep walking."

She glanced toward the stream. "We can follow the water. It'll hide our tracks."

Lukas gave a tired half-smile. "Always thinking like a soldier."

"Like a nurse who doesn't want to treat another gunshot," she corrected, pulling her cloak around her.

They stepped out of the chapel together. Mist hung low between the trees, the kind of morning where every sound carried far. As they followed the stream's curve, the sun broke weakly through the fog — a faint, cold gleam that caught the edge of something ahead.

Anna stopped. "Lukas... do you see that?"

A shape crouched beside the water, half-hidden in reeds. At first, she thought it was an animal. Then it moved — a man, thin and trembling, his clothes torn and muddied. His hands clutched a bundle close to his chest.

Lukas raised a hand in warning. "Stay behind me."

But when they stepped closer, the man looked up — his face gaunt, eyes wide with terror. He was older, perhaps fifty, with a gray stubble and the hollow look of someone long afraid.

"Don't come closer," he rasped. "I've done nothing — nothing!"

Anna froze. "We're not soldiers," she said quickly, her voice low, soothing. "We won't hurt you."

The man's gaze darted between them, then toward the forest behind. "They're coming," he whispered. "The patrol —

they shot the others. They said the bridge was sabotaged, that we were spies. I ran."

Lukas crouched carefully, keeping his hands visible. "What bridge?"

"Downstream," the man said, shaking. "Two nights ago, it blew apart. They blamed anyone nearby — farmers, travelers. I saw them drag people away."

Anna's heart sank. "My parents—"

"I don't know names," the man said. "But they've set posts along the river. They're looking for anyone without papers."

He clutched the bundle tighter — a child's coat, Anna realized, though there was no child with him.

"She didn't wake up," he said softly, voice breaking. "The shelling… I couldn't—"

Anna knelt beside him before he could finish, her hand resting lightly on his arm. "I'm sorry," she whispered.

The man looked at her, eyes wet and wild. "You can't go east," he said. "The patrols are thick. But west — across the ridge — there's an old mill. Empty now. You can hide there. The soldiers won't search that far; they think it's cursed."

Lukas met Anna's eyes. "A cursed mill sounds safer than the front line."

She nodded. "Can you make it that far?" she asked the man.

He shook his head. "No. I'll wait here. Maybe they'll pass me by."

Anna wanted to protest, but Lukas's hand touched her shoulder. He gave the man his flask of water, then helped Anna to her feet.

"Thank you," Lukas said quietly. "We'll remember this."

The man only nodded, his gaze drifting to the bundle in his arms. As they turned away, Anna looked back once — the figure hunched in the mist, small and broken, yet somehow unbowed.

They followed the stream westward, the forest thickening around them once more. Behind them, faint and far, came the echo of voices — the soldiers again, searching the riverbank. But ahead, through the fog, Anna thought she saw a darker shape rising from the trees — a tall, crooked silhouette against the paling sky.

"Lukas," she whispered. "The mill."

He followed her gaze, nodding. "Then that's where we go."

And together, with the mist closing behind them and the war still stalking their heels, they made for the ruin that might yet be their salvation.

CHAPTER SEVENTEEN:
The Old Mill

The path to the mill wound upward through a tangle of pine and birch. The mist thinned as they climbed, giving way to the skeletal outline of the building—black timbers rising crookedly from the hillside, the shattered sails of its wheel sagging over the stream like broken wings. Moss climbed the stone foundation; the windows were glassless, yawning dark against the gray sky.

Anna hesitated at the edge of the clearing. The air here felt different, still and heavy, as though the forest itself had stopped breathing.

"It's beautiful," she said quietly, "and terrible."

Lukas leaned on his crutch, studying the ruin. "It'll keep the rain out. That's enough beauty for me."

They crossed the threshold carefully. The wooden floor creaked beneath their weight. Inside, dust lay thick over everything—old sacks of grain, a rusted pulley, the skeletal remains of a millstone cracked in half. Water trickled faintly somewhere beneath the floorboards, the slow heartbeat of the stream that had once turned the wheel.

A faded crucifix hung crooked over the doorway, one arm missing. Cobwebs veiled the corners, trembling slightly as they passed. The air smelled of mildew, iron, and something faintly sweet—perhaps the ghost of flour long since gone.

Lukas set his pack down and struck a match. The tiny flame flared gold, catching the edges of the room. "There's an upper floor," he said. "Looks stable enough. We can rest there."

They climbed the narrow stairs, the boards groaning underfoot. At the top was a small loft with a single window overlooking the stream. Through it, the dying light of evening spilled in, soft and amber. Dust motes drifted in the beam like slow-moving snow.

Anna dropped her satchel on a crate and sat, shoulders sagging. "It's the first roof that hasn't leaked in days."

Lukas sank down opposite her, his back against the wall. For a while, neither spoke. The silence of the place was strange—thick, echoing. Every breath, every movement seemed too loud.

Finally, Anna said, "Do you believe what he told us? That the soldiers won't come here because they think it's cursed?"

Lukas looked toward the window, where the last light was fading. "Every soldier believes in something that keeps him alive. Maybe that's enough."

As night fell, the forest grew quiet except for the occasional drip of water and the groan of the old beams in the wind. Anna lit a small lamp, its glow barely reaching the walls. She spread her cloak over Lukas's shoulders where he sat dozing, his face drawn and pale. The sight of him stirred something deep and aching in her chest—relief, fear, and a tenderness too fragile to name.

Outside, an owl called once. The sound echoed through the rafters, low and mournful.

Anna shivered. "It feels as if someone's still here," she murmured.

Lukas opened his eyes, the lamplight catching the blue-gray of them. "Maybe just the people who left pieces of themselves behind."

He gestured to the far corner, where a child's shoe lay half-buried in dust, its leather curled and cracked. Nearby, a rusted spoon, a threadbare blanket. Lives interrupted. Anna rose and knelt beside the shoe, brushing away the dirt with her fingers.

"They fled, too," she whispered. "Long before us."

Lukas's voice was soft behind her. "The war always finds new ghosts."

She turned back to him, the lamplight trembling in her hands. "Do you think it'll end, Lukas? Truly end?"

He looked away, his jaw tightening. "I used to. Now I think it just changes shape."

They sat in silence again, the mill sighing around them. Wind slipped through the cracks, making the beams creak like old bones. The faint smell of smoke drifted in from the hearth below—something ancient burning out of sight.

Anna drew her knees to her chest, staring into the dimness. The shadows seemed to move there, slow and deliberate, as if remembering the hands that had built this place. She thought of her parents, of the message that had condemned them, and felt the guilt settle like a stone in her stomach.

Lukas stirred, his voice barely audible. "You did what you had to. You can't carry all of it."

She looked at him sharply. "Were you awake?"

A faint smile ghosted across his lips. "Long enough to hear you thinking."

Despite herself, she smiled back—small, trembling, but real. The lamplight between them flickered once, then steadied. Outside, the wind rose and fell, carrying with it the endless murmur of the river.

For the first time in days, neither of them spoke of running. The ghosts could whisper, the beams could creak—but for one fragile night, they belonged to the quiet.

The lamp burned low, its circle of light shrinking until it barely touched the walls. Beyond it, the rest of the loft dissolved into shadow. The storm had passed, but the wind still prowled around the old mill, brushing the timbers with a hollow moan.

Anna could not sleep. Every time she closed her eyes, she saw flashes of the camp—the inspectors, the letter, her parents 'faces when the soldiers came. She sat with her back against the wall, listening to the slow rhythm of Lukas's breathing across the small space. Each rise and fall steadied her a little more.

When he spoke, his voice came low, rough with exhaustion. "You're still awake."

"So are you."

A pause, then a faint smile she could hear even in the dark.

"I can feel you thinking again."

"I was trying not to."

He shifted slightly, the wood creaking beneath him. "Does it help, running?"

She hugged her knees tighter. "I don't know anymore. Maybe we're just buying time."

"Time's all anyone ever buys."

The words hung there, quiet and true. After a while, she reached for the lamp, trimming the wick to keep it alive. The small act filled the room with a softer glow, enough for her to see him more clearly—the bruise at his temple, the stubborn set of his mouth, the tension still coiled in his shoulders.

"You should lie down," she said. "You need to heal."

"And leave you to guard the ghosts?"

"I think they'd prefer me. I'm gentler."

That earned the faintest laugh from him, half sigh, half warmth. He leaned his head back against the beam. "You've seen me at my worst, Anna Müller. I'm not sure you should still sound that kind."

"You've seen me afraid," she answered quietly. "And you didn't turn away."

The silence that followed wasn't heavy now—it pulsed with something unspoken, steady as a heartbeat. Lukas reached for his canteen, then hesitated halfway, his hand falling instead to the floor between them. Slowly, without meeting her eyes, he opened it toward her.

She placed her hand in his. Their fingers fit together clumsily at first, then easily, palms warming in the chill air. For a moment, neither moved. The lamp hissed softly; somewhere below, the river whispered against the stones.

"Do you ever wish," he murmured, "that we'd met before all this? Before uniforms and wounds and lies?"

"All the time," she said. "But maybe we wouldn't have seen each other then. Not like this."

He turned toward her, and for the first time that night, the fear in his eyes eased. He brushed a stray curl from her cheek with the back of his hand. His touch was hesitant, almost reverent, as if she might vanish if he reached too quickly.

"You're freezing," he said.

"So are you."

He shifted his coat, spreading it across both their shoulders. The gesture drew them close, close enough that she could feel the warmth of his breath on her skin. Outside, the wind dropped away, leaving only the pulse of the river and the faint ticking of the cooling lamp.

They sat like that for a long time—two fugitives wrapped in one coat, neither sure what tomorrow would bring. Anna rested her head against his shoulder; he let out a slow breath and leaned lightly into her.

When she finally spoke, it was barely more than a whisper.

"I'm afraid of what comes next."

"Me too," he admitted. "But if we wake up tomorrow, we'll face it. Together."

The words were simple, but they reached deeper than any promise. She closed her eyes, listening to his heartbeat, feeling the tremor in his fingers fade. The mill groaned softly, settling into the quiet.

Just before dawn, the first gray light touched the window. Anna stirred, half dreaming, and realized that Lukas's arm had fallen around her shoulders. She did not move it. For a brief, trembling moment, she allowed herself to believe that peace could exist, even here—between breaths, between battles.

Outside, the forest exhaled. Another day was coming. But inside the ruined mill, the war felt a world away.

CHAPTER EIGHTEEN:
The Choice

The morning came pale and sharp, sunlight cutting through the mist like a blade. The air smelled of pine and damp stone; the world outside the mill seemed washed clean by the storm. For the first time in days, the guns were silent.

Anna woke to that silence and, for a moment, let herself believe it meant peace. Lukas was still asleep beside her, his coat pulled up to his chin, the faintest color back in his face. She sat quietly, watching the light shift across the floorboards. Dust floated in the sunbeams like drifting ash.

But then—far off, carried faintly through the trees—came the low growl of engines.

She froze. Not thunder. Trucks.

Anna shook Lukas awake, her hand gripping his shoulder. "They're coming."

He blinked, groggy at first, then alert. The sound grew louder, joined by the metallic clatter of weapons, the bark of orders shouted in German.

Lukas was already pulling on his coat, wincing as he tested his leg. "They've tracked us. Maybe from the riverbank."

Anna looked toward the narrow window. Down the slope, shapes were moving between the trees—dark uniforms, the flash of rifles, a banner of exhaust drifting through the branches.

Her throat tightened. "We can't outrun them."

"No," Lukas said, scanning the room. "But we can outthink them."

He crossed to the back wall, where a trapdoor sagged half-hidden beneath a pile of rotted sacks. He knelt, wrenching it open with a splintering groan. Beneath lay a narrow space— an old storage pit, half-collapsed, deep enough for one, maybe two if they didn't breathe too loudly. The smell of earth and mold wafted up.

"Get in," he said.

"Lukas—"

"Now, Anna. If they find me, they might not look twice. But if they find you—"

"I'm not leaving you here."

Their eyes met in the dim light. For a heartbeat, neither moved. The shouts outside drew closer—boots pounding over wet leaves.

"They'll kill you," she whispered.

"They'll do worse to you," he said. "Please."

She hesitated, then shook her head. "No. If we're caught, we're caught together."

He stared at her—half disbelief, half fierce, aching admiration. "You stubborn woman."

A window shattered downstairs. Voices echoed through the lower floor. Lukas grabbed her hand. "Then come."

He limped toward the back of the mill, where the remains of the water wheel jutted into the ravine. The gears beneath the broken platform still turned weakly with the flow, grinding slow and heavy. "There," he said, pointing to the far side of the ravine where dense trees cloaked the hillside. "If we can cross the wheel, we'll lose them in the forest."

Anna looked down—the drop was steep, the current below fast and black. "It'll never hold both of us."

"We don't need both of us on it at once." He set his crutch aside, tightening the strap on his satchel. "Go first. When you're across, I'll follow."

A shout split the air—closer now, inside the mill. Boots thudded on the stairs.

Anna swallowed hard, then stepped onto the broken wheel. The wood was slick beneath her boots; water splashed her skirts as she moved. The wheel creaked, sagged, but held. She gripped the iron spokes and pulled herself across, heart hammering.

Halfway, she looked back. Lukas stood at the edge, rifle in hand—one he'd snatched from the ruins below. The expression on his face was calm, almost eerily so.

"Lukas, come on!"

He nodded once, then turned as the first soldier burst into the loft, shouting orders. Anna's cry caught in her throat. The soldier fired—the shot cracked through the mill, splintering the beam beside Lukas's head.

Lukas fired back. The man fell. Another shout answered from below.

Anna reached the far side, hauling herself up onto the muddy bank. "Lukas!" she screamed over the roar of the stream.

He slung the rifle over his shoulder and limped to the wheel, grabbing a support beam as bullets tore through the wall behind him. The wheel groaned under his weight. Water sprayed his face; he slipped, caught himself, kept moving.

"Don't look back," he called. "Run when I reach you."

"Not without you."

A crack of gunfire—splinters flew, and Lukas stumbled, his leg buckling. For a heartbeat, Anna thought he would fall into the churning water, but his hand shot out, gripping the iron rung. He pulled himself forward, teeth gritted in pain.

She reached down as he neared the bank, fingers outstretched. Their hands met—mud, water, blood—and she dragged him the last distance. They fell together onto the wet ground, breathless, shaking.

Behind them, shouts rose. The soldiers had reached the broken platform. Anna could see their shapes in the mist, rifles raised.

Lukas grabbed her hand. "Now we run."

They plunged into the trees. Branches whipped their faces, the ground a blur beneath their feet. Behind them came the muffled crash of the wheel collapsing under gunfire, the roar of the river swallowing the sound.

They didn't stop until the forest swallowed all trace of the mill. Lukas leaned against a tree, gasping, his hand pressed to his side where blood seeped through his coat.

Anna turned to him, trembling. "You're hit."

He shook his head, though his face was gray. "Just grazed."

"Sit down—let me see."

He managed a weak smile. "You said that the first night we met."

She almost laughed, but the sound broke into a sob instead. Kneeling beside him, she pressed her hands over the wound, her tears mixing with the blood and rain.

"You saved us," she whispered.

"You keep saying *us*," he murmured, his eyes fluttering. "I'm starting to believe it."

From somewhere far behind, the faint echo of shouting drifted through the trees. Lukas's eyes met hers.

"They'll keep hunting," he said softly. "We have to keep moving."

Anna nodded, tightening her hold on him. "Then we move. Together."

The forest stretched ahead—endless, dark, and unknown. But as the sun broke weakly through the canopy, casting a golden haze over the wet leaves, Anna felt something stir deep inside: not peace, not safety, but the fierce, unyielding will to survive.

And as Lukas leaned on her shoulder and they began their slow walk into the light, the ruins of the mill faded behind them—another ghost swallowed by the forest, another secret the war would never tell.

* * *

By nightfall, the forest had turned to ink. The sky was a low lid of cloud, no stars, no moon—only the faint hiss of wind through the pines and the dull ache of exhaustion pressing on them both.

They had walked until Lukas could walk no more. Now he sat slumped against a tree, one arm wrapped around his ribs, his breath shallow. Blood had soaked through the crude bandage Anna had tied hours before; it glistened darkly when she lifted the lamp to look.

The sight hollowed her. "It's worse," she whispered.

"It's nothing," he said, though the effort of speaking made his voice tremble.

"Don't lie to me, Lukas."

He tried for a smile but couldn't hold it. The color had drained from his face. Sweat beaded his forehead despite the cold.

They'd found a small hollow under an overhang of rock—a shallow cave where the earth was dry. Anna had kindled a small fire from twigs and bark, just enough to warm her hands. The smoke curled faintly toward the opening. It wasn't much shelter, but it was all they had.

She knelt beside him, cutting away the bloodied cloth with her scissors. The wound along his side was ragged, the bullet having grazed deep through muscle. It had missed the lung by luck alone, but infection was already setting in—the edges hot and angry beneath her fingertips.

"I have to clean it again," she said.

He nodded once, eyes shut. "Do it."

She poured water over the wound. He hissed, biting down hard on his sleeve. The smell of blood filled the narrow space. Anna's hands didn't tremble—she'd done this too many times—but her chest hurt with every sound he made.

When it was clean, she pressed a strip of morphine and fresh linen against it, tying the bandage tight. He sagged back, breathing raggedly. For a moment, the only sound was the crackle of the tiny fire.

"You need rest," she said softly.

"No time," he murmured. "They'll be moving at dawn. We have to—"

"You won't live to see dawn if you don't rest."

He opened his eyes then, and in the dim light they looked distant—fever-bright. "If I sleep, I might not wake."

Anna froze. The thought had already crossed her mind, but hearing it aloud tore at her. She reached for his hand, feeling how cold it was.

"You will," she said. "Because I won't let you go."

He gave a faint laugh that turned into a cough. Blood spotted his lips. "You're still trying to save everyone."

"Only one, tonight," she whispered.

His gaze softened, and he lifted a shaking hand to brush her cheek. "If you have to run—"

"Don't." Her voice broke. "Don't you dare tell me to leave you."

"If they find us, you can still—"

"I said no."

She took his face in her hands, forcing him to meet her eyes. "I've seen too much death. I won't add yours to it."

For a heartbeat, neither of them breathed. The firelight flickered between them, painting his face in shifting gold and shadow.

Then she saw it—the distant look of someone slipping, the fever dragging him under. His pulse fluttered weakly beneath her fingers.

She rummaged through her satchel, desperate. Only one dose of morphine left. It would ease his pain—but too much, and he might never wake. Without it, the pain alone could drive him past endurance.

Her hand hovered over the vial. A nurse's instincts battled the woman's terror inside her.

"Lukas," she whispered. "Stay with me."

He stirred faintly. "Do it," he breathed. "Please."

Anna's eyes filled. "If I give you this, you might not wake."

"Then I'll trust you to bring me back."

Her throat closed. She drew the dose carefully, her fingers steady even as tears blurred her vision. She pressed the needle into his arm, whispering, "Forgive me," as she pushed the plunger down.

He shuddered once, then exhaled, his body easing as the pain ebbed away. His hand found hers, squeezing weakly.

"*Vielen Dank*," he murmured, eyes closing.

She sat with him long after, counting each breath, each flicker of movement, terrified of the moment when they might stop. The fire dimmed to embers, painting his face in soft red light.

At last, she leaned forward, resting her forehead against his shoulder. "Don't leave me," she whispered. "Please don't."

Outside, the forest whispered in the wind. The scent of rain and pine drifted in through the narrow gap of the cave. She sat through the long hours, her hand never leaving his, willing his pulse to keep beating.

Lukas stirred faintly, a sound escaping his lips—hoarse, but alive. Anna's breath caught. She leaned closer, tears falling freely now, "You came back."

He blinked at her, the faintest ghost of a smile touching his mouth. "You said you wouldn't let me go."

Relief flooded her so sharply it hurt. She pressed her hand against his chest, feeling the slow, stubborn beat of his heart.

She leaned down and kissed him gently on the lips. "Sleep again, *mein Lieber.*"

And as the first light filtered through the trees outside, Anna realized the war had taken nearly everything from them—but not this. Not yet. She closed her eyes and slept.

* * *

The cave was little more than a hollow in the hillside, damp and smelling of earth and stone. Outside, mist curled low across the valley, carrying the chill of early morning. Anna woke to the sound of Lukas breathing — ragged, uneven, every breath catching in his chest.

162

She touched his forehead. It burned beneath her hand. The fever was back — worse than before.

"Lukas," she whispered, shaking him gently. "Lukas, can you hear me?"

He stirred faintly, eyes half-open. His lips moved but no words came, only a hoarse sound that broke her heart. She pulled the coat tighter around him, pressing her cheek to his.

"You'll be all right," she whispered, even as fear clawed at her throat. "I won't let anything happen to you."

But he was far too weak to move, and they had nothing left — no bread, no water, no medicine. The small pouch of bandages was empty save for one strip, already stained.

Anna rose, tucking the coat more securely around him, and looked toward the mouth of the cave. The sky outside was the color of pewter. She hesitated — afraid to leave him, afraid *not* to.

"I'll be right back," she said softly. "I promise. Don't you dare stop breathing."

He gave no reply, only a faint tremor of his hand against hers. She pressed his fingers to her lips, then slipped out into the cold.

The world beyond the cave was silent except for the drip of melting frost. Anna stumbled through the undergrowth, searching for any sign of a stream. Her boots were soaked, her hands numb, but she forced herself on. Every step she thought of his face — the fever flush, the shallow breaths — and it drove her forward.

At last, she found a trickle of water running down the rocks, clear and cold. She cupped it in her hands and drank, then filled a dented tin she'd scavenged from the road days before.

Food was harder. She dug through fallen leaves, found a few wild mushrooms, and gathered them carefully, praying they were the kind she remembered from childhood walks with her father. She tore up some roots, too — bitter, but edible.

When she returned to the cave, Lukas was shivering violently, his face deathly pale beneath the fever's sheen.

"Lukas!" She dropped to her knees beside him, setting down the water and shaking his shoulders. "Stay with me, please."

His eyes fluttered open. "Anna…"

She gave a choked laugh of relief. "Yes, I'm here." She lifted his head, letting a few drops of water touch his lips. "Just a little."

He swallowed weakly, then winced. "You shouldn't… be out there alone."

"Don't talk." She brushed back his damp hair. "Save your strength. That's my job now."

He tried to smile but it faltered. His hand found hers again, cold and trembling. "You always come back."

"Always," she whispered, her eyes stinging. "Even if I have to walk through the whole damned war to find you."

She laid the coat over him again, fed him another sip of water, then gathered kindling from the dry corner of the cave.

Her hands shook so badly it took three tries to strike the match, but when the small flame finally caught, she nearly wept with relief.

The warmth flickered across the stone walls, painting their shadows together. She cradled Lukas's head in her lap, humming under her breath — a tune she half-remembered from home.

"Sleep, *mein Lieber*," she murmured. "Rest. I'll keep watch."

Outside, the mist thickened, hiding them from the world. Inside the cave, the tiny fire crackled, and in its fragile glow, Anna held on — to him, to hope, to the faint promise that morning might still bring life.

CHAPTER NINETEEN:
The Edge of Hope

The fire had burned down to its faintest glow, little more than a bed of coals whispering in the gray light. Dawn crept softly over the trees, pale and colorless, the first birdcalls tentative and unsure. The forest smelled of wet moss and smoke.

Anna hadn't slept. She sat slumped beside Lukas, her hand still resting against his chest, counting each steady rise and fall as if the rhythm alone could keep him tethered to the world. When he stirred at last, she straightened instantly.

"Lukas?"

He blinked, eyes unfocused for a moment before finding her. "Still here." His voice was raw but alive.

"Still here," she said, smiling through her exhaustion.

He shifted, wincing. "How long?"

"All night. You scared me."

"That makes us even."

He tried to sit up. Anna caught his shoulder. "Don't. You're too weak."

"We can't stay, Anna. If patrols circle back—"

"Then we'll move when you can stand."

He turned his head toward the cave mouth where light slanted through the leaves. "It's morning already."

"Ja."

"Then help me up."

Reluctantly, she slid her arm under his and helped him rise. He swayed, leaning heavily against her. She felt the weight of him, the heat still radiating from the fever, but there was strength there too—just enough.

They stepped out into the forest. Dew clung to every leaf, sparkling faintly in the pale light. The river's distant murmur drifted through the trees. Lukas paused, drawing a slow breath as if relearning the air itself.

"We survived the night," he murmured.

Anna squeezed his hand. "And we survive the day."

They began walking north, following the faint game trail that wound between the birches. Each step cost Lukas visible effort, but he said nothing. The forest was waking around them—small sounds of life returning, the first weak sunlight touching the tops of the trees.

For the first time in days, Anna felt something like hope. Fragile, yes—but real.

By midmorning, the mist had lifted, and the forest was all gold and green. They stopped at a shallow stream to drink. Lukas knelt, cupping the cold water to his lips, and Anna washed the blood from her hands. The moment was quiet, almost ordinary.

Then a twig snapped nearby.

Anna froze. Lukas's hand went instantly to the knife at his belt. They both turned toward the sound.

A figure stepped from behind the trees—a man in a long, tattered coat, his hair cropped short, a rifle slung over one shoulder. His boots were caked with mud, and his eyes, sharp and wary, fixed on them.

"Don't move," he said in German.

Anna's heart seized. She lifted her hands slowly. "We're not soldiers."

"No?" He tilted his head. "Then what are you doing this deep in the forest?"

Lukas straightened with effort, his stance steady despite the injury. "Escaping the war."

The man studied him for a long moment, then shifted the rifle slightly—but didn't lower it. "You're the nurse," he said finally. "And the soldier. They've been looking for you."

Anna's breath caught. "Then you know who we are?"

He nodded. "Everyone along the river knows. Word travels faster than bullets these days."

Lukas's hand tightened around the knife. "Then what are you? A bounty hunter?"

The man's mouth curved into a faint smile. "No. Something better."

He slung the rifle off his shoulder and set it against a tree, raising both hands. "Name's Emil Kovács. I work with the *Résistance*—the local cell near Saint-Véron. We heard of a nurse and a German deserter heading west. Some say you burned a letter meant for Command."

168

Anna exchanged a glance with Lukas. "You believe everything you hear?" she asked cautiously.

"Not everything," Emil said. "But enough to know you're running for your lives. And that you might be worth saving."

Lukas frowned. "Why help us?"

Emil shrugged. "Because you're both enemies of the same men who've killed too many of mine." His tone softened slightly. "We have a safe house not far from here. Food. Medicine. A way to cross the border if you're careful."

Anna's heart began to race again—not from fear this time, but the dizzying pulse of possibility. "A safe house?"

"Old vineyard cellar, north of here. Half a day's walk."

Lukas hesitated. "If this is a trap—"

"You'll know soon enough," Emil said. "But if you stay here, you won't live to find out."

The forest fell quiet again, only the stream murmuring between them. Anna looked at Lukas, seeing the exhaustion etched deep into his face, the pain he was trying to hide. There was no choice.

"We'll come," she said.

Emil nodded, shouldering his rifle. "Then stay close. And don't speak unless I tell you."

He started up the trail without looking back. Lukas met Anna's gaze, half wary, half resigned.

"Do we trust him?"

"We have to," she said.

He gave a small nod, and together they followed. The forest swallowed their footsteps as the sun climbed higher, burning away the last of the mist. For the first time, their path no longer led deeper into darkness—but toward the faint, uncertain light of something like freedom.

The forest thickened as they walked north. The trees grew closer together, their branches tangled like dark ribs overhead, and the sunlight came in fractured patterns, glinting off wet leaves and stones. Emil moved ahead of them with the quiet ease of someone born to the woods, each step deliberate, each pause measured.

Lukas leaned heavier on his crutch with every mile, his face drawn tight with pain, though he never complained. Anna stayed close to him, steadying him when the trail grew steep or slick. Neither spoke. The air felt heavy with listening things— the creak of trees, the echo of distant gunfire far to the east, the low rumble of thunder somewhere beyond the ridge.

After an hour, Emil lifted a hand for silence. He crouched beside a fallen log, scanning the slope below.

"Patrol road," he murmured. "They move supplies between the river and Saint-Véron. We'll cross above the bend."

Anna followed his gaze. Through the trees below, the faint shimmer of a dirt road cut through the forest. The tracks of trucks and boots were carved deep in the mud. She could hear it now—a faint rhythmic grind, the rumble of engines approaching.

"We should wait," Lukas whispered.

Emil shook his head. "Too exposed here. We move while the trucks are still distant. Quickly."

They began to climb, boots slipping in the wet soil. Lukas's breath came ragged, each step a struggle. Anna felt his weight against her as they reached the ridge, hearts pounding.

The first truck appeared below, crawling along the road, a red cross painted hastily on its side. A decoy. Soldiers walked beside it, rifles slung over their shoulders. Anna could make out their voices—lazy, half-joking, oblivious to the fugitives just above them.

They waited, pressed flat against the earth until the sound faded. Emil gave a quick signal, and they began moving again. But before they reached the next rise, a sharp crack split the air.

Not thunder. Gunfire.

A second shot, closer. Bark exploded from the tree beside Lukas's head.

"Down!" Emil hissed.

They dove behind a fallen trunk as bullets tore through the underbrush. The shouts came from below—half a dozen men, maybe more. A patrol.

"How did they find us?" Anna gasped.

Emil cursed under his breath. "They must have seen our tracks by the stream. Stay low."

He raised his rifle, sighted down the slope, and fired. The crack echoed through the forest, followed by a scream. Lukas gritted his teeth, pressing his shoulder against the log, his knuckles white around the knife hilt.

"Anna," he said quietly, "if they flank us—"

"Don't," she cut him off. "We're getting out of this."

The air filled with smoke and the reek of gunpowder. Emil reloaded quickly, firing again. A bullet struck the log inches from Anna's hand, splintering the wood. She ducked, heart hammering. The sound of boots was closer now—men shouting orders in German.

Emil turned to Lukas. "There's a ravine ahead. If we break right and run, they'll lose line of sight. I'll cover you."

"You'll be killed," Anna protested.

"Only if you waste the chance."

Another burst of gunfire answered him. Emil's jaw tightened. "Go!"

Lukas grabbed Anna's hand, pulling her up. They ran, stumbling through mud and roots, the forest erupting behind them. Branches whipped at their faces, the crack of rifles chasing them through the trees. Lukas's limp slowed them, but he refused to stop. Anna could hear her own breath in her ears, loud and ragged, the thud of her heartbeat drowning everything else.

They broke through the underbrush and saw it—the ravine, narrow but steep, filled with ferns and loose stones. Lukas hesitated only a second before jumping. He hit hard, rolling once, his crutch snapping beneath him. Anna scrambled down after him, half-falling, half-sliding.

They landed in the damp hollow, panting, and the noise of pursuit dimmed above. Anna crawled to Lukas's side. His face was pale, his leg bent awkwardly. "Can you stand?"

"Not quickly," he admitted, his breath sharp. "But we have to keep moving."

She looked up the slope. Emil was still on the ridge, firing in short bursts to draw the soldiers 'fire away from them. One bullet struck close; he ducked behind a tree, then glanced down at them.

"Run!" he shouted. "Follow the creek north!"

Anna wanted to scream at him to come with them, but Lukas tugged her arm. "He's right. Go!"

They stumbled through the ravine, following the stream as it twisted through the rocks. Behind them, the gunfire slowed, replaced by scattered shouts. Then, somewhere above, came the unmistakable explosion of a grenade—and the echoing collapse of silence.

Anna froze mid-step. Lukas turned, his expression grim. The sound that followed was faint and final.

Neither spoke. They kept moving, the forest closing around them again.

By the time they stopped, the sky was darkening once more. Lukas sank to the ground, breathless, his broken crutch lying in the mud. Anna knelt beside him, pressing her forehead to his shoulder.

"He saved us," she whispered.

Lukas nodded slowly, his hand finding hers. "Then we'll make it mean something."

They sat in silence, the forest quiet except for the wind. Somewhere ahead lay the safe house, or what was left of it— another ghost of promise in a world still burning. But even amid the ache and the loss, Anna felt the ember of something stubborn inside her, a resolve that refused to die.

"We keep moving," she said at last.

"Until when?" Lukas asked softly.

She met his eyes. "Until there's nowhere left to run—or until we find a place to live."

He gave a weary nod. "Then let's find it."

And together, beneath the bleeding light of another evening, they rose and vanished into the forest's long, echoing quiet.

CHAPTER TWENTY:
The Resistance Safe House

Night had long since fallen by the time Anna and Lukas reached the edge of the valley. The forest opened into rolling fields half-swallowed by mist, and in the hollow below stood the remains of a vineyard—rows of broken posts and dead vines stretching like ribs toward the horizon. The air was heavy with damp earth and smoke from some distant fire.

At the heart of the ruin stood a stone farmhouse, roof sagging, one window faintly lit. Beyond it, the black mouth of a cellar yawned open—its doorway half-hidden behind a tangle of ivy. Anna hesitated at the sight. After days of running, the place looked less like safety and more like another grave waiting to be filled.

Lukas leaned against her shoulder, limping heavily now that his makeshift crutch was little more than a splintered stick. His face was pale beneath the dirt, his breath shallow. "If this is another trap…" he murmured.

Anna squeezed his arm gently. "It's all we have left."

They moved cautiously down the slope, keeping low between the rows of dead vines. The lamp in the farmhouse flickered, then went dark. For a moment, only the wind moved through the field. Then—a voice, low and sharp in French.

"Arrêtez-vous là."

A silhouette appeared by the cellar door, rifle raised. Another followed—two men, both in rough clothes, their faces masked by scarves. One of them stepped forward, calling again:

"Nom et raison."

Anna froze, her heart thudding. Before she could speak, another voice came from behind the soldiers, older, measured.

"Enough, Pierre. If they made it here, they're either fools or desperate. Let's see which."

The speaker stepped into the lamplight, a woman this time—tall, her hair bound beneath a kerchief, eyes keen and dark. She studied them for a long moment before lowering her weapon slightly.

"You're the nurse," she said in accented German. "And you—" her gaze shifted to Lukas "—the soldier who turned his back on the Reich."

Lukas met her eyes. "We didn't come to fight you. We came to survive."

The woman gave a small, humorless smile. "That makes three of us." She turned to the others. "Bring them in. Quickly."

The cellar was deeper than it appeared from the outside. Narrow steps led down into a wide, low chamber lit by two oil lamps. The air smelled of wine and dust. Crates lined the walls, and a long wooden table sat in the center, cluttered with maps, a radio, and a scattering of tin cups.

Anna helped Lukas down the last steps, her arm steady around him. The woman followed, shutting the heavy door above them. "My name is Claire Duval," she said. "You met Emil, I think."

Anna's throat tightened. "We did. He… he didn't make it."

Claire's expression didn't change, though something flickered briefly in her eyes. "I thought as much. He was good

176

at dying for causes. Less good at living for them." She gestured to a bench. "Sit. You're safe here, for now."

Anna eased Lukas onto the bench. The warmth of the cellar hit her like a wave; her legs almost gave out from exhaustion. Claire poured water into a cup and handed it to her.

"Drink. You look half-dead."

Anna took it gratefully, then glanced around the room. A man worked at the far table, tuning the radio with careful hands. Another sorted through a stack of papers, murmuring to himself. None of them looked surprised to see new faces—only wary.

"This is the Saint-Véron cell," Claire said. "What's left of it. Five of us, sometimes six when the others return. Emil said you could help us."

Lukas frowned. "Help you? We've barely survived the last week."

"You're both more useful than you think," Claire replied. "A nurse who knows the front's procedures, a soldier who knows their patrol routes—knowledge like that saves lives." She leaned forward slightly. "And before he died, Emil said you carried something the Germans were desperate to find. A letter?"

Anna felt her heart stop. "It was destroyed."

"But they think otherwise," Claire said. "Their search teams are spreading west from the river. They're calling it a matter of national betrayal." Her eyes softened a fraction. "You've already changed their plans just by surviving."

Lukas glanced at Anna, his brow furrowed. "If we stay here, they'll find you too."

Claire shrugged. "They already know we exist. The only question is how long we can make that matter."

She stood, turning toward the stairwell. "Rest. Eat. I'll post a watch. At dawn we'll talk again—about what comes next."

When she was gone, the cellar fell quiet except for the faint hum of the radio. Anna sank beside Lukas, exhaustion pressing down like a weight. For the first time in days, the air didn't smell of blood or gunpowder. She looked at him, the tension easing from her shoulders.

"Do you think we can trust them?" she asked softly.

Lukas closed his eyes, his head tipping back against the wall. "I don't know. But it feels good not to run."

Anna smiled faintly, brushing a damp lock of hair from his forehead. "Then maybe we rest tonight. Just this once."

He nodded, his voice barely above a whisper. "Just this once."

The lamps burned low, casting long shadows over the maps and rifles and the faces of strangers who might soon be comrades— or casualties. Somewhere above them, the war pressed on. But below, in that hidden hollow beneath the earth, two fugitives finally exhaled.

The night stretched quiet and uncertain, holding its breath for whatever the morning would bring.

* * *

A pale light filtered through the cracks in the cellar door, turning the dust in the air to faint silver. Someone upstairs was moving quietly, the scrape of boots on floorboards followed by the smell of coffee and wood smoke drifting down. The hum of the small radio filled the underground room with a soft, nervous pulse.

Anna woke with a start. For a moment, she didn't remember where she was. Then the rough stone ceiling above her came into focus, and she felt Lukas's warmth beside her. He was still asleep, his breathing even, one hand resting lightly on the edge of the blanket Claire had thrown over them during the night.

The last traces of fever had faded from his skin. Relief rippled through her chest. They'd survived the night again.

The cellar door creaked open, and Claire's voice cut softly through the stillness.

"You can both wake. We have work to discuss."

Anna rose carefully, rubbing the stiffness from her neck. Lukas stirred and blinked, pushing himself upright with a wince. The first hint of morning reached the steps behind Claire, framing her in cold light. She held a rolled map under her arm.

"Come upstairs," she said. "It's safer to speak before the others return."

The farmhouse kitchen was dim and spare, the table cleared except for the map spread across it. A single oil lamp burned beside it, its flame steady. Claire stood at the head of the table, her sleeves rolled, her eyes sharp with purpose. She gestured for them to sit.

"We're cut off from the main resistance line," she began. "Our contact in Lyon hasn't transmitted in five days. We believe the radio operator was captured."

She pointed to a red mark on the map—a village emblem drawn near the foothills to the west.

"There's a German communications post here, outside Saint-Véron. They're intercepting our messages, tracing them back to cells like this one. We've already lost three safe houses because of it. If we don't destroy that transmitter, they'll find this place within a week."

Anna leaned forward, the scent of coffee mingling with the paper and ink. "You want us to help destroy it?"

"We need someone who can get inside," Claire said. "The post is disguised as a medical depot. A nurse and a wounded soldier would draw less suspicion than armed partisans."

Lukas stiffened. "You want us to walk straight into a German garrison?"

"Yes," Claire replied simply. "You speak the language. You know their manner, their paperwork, their uniforms. You could pass long enough to plant the charges."

Anna's stomach twisted. "And if they recognize us?"

Claire met her eyes without flinching. "Then you'll die quickly, and perhaps the rest of us will live a little longer."

For a long moment, no one spoke. The only sound was the faint crackle of the lamp.

Lukas broke the silence. "You'd risk the last of your people on one explosion?"

"Not a risk," Claire said. "A necessity. If we cut their lines, it buys time for every cell between here and Lyon."

She reached into her coat and drew out a folded armband, the kind marked with the red cross of field medics. It was stained and frayed.

"You'll wear this," she said, handing it to Anna. "We have a wagon and a driver who can take you within three kilometers of the depot. After that, you're on your own."

Anna's hands trembled as she took the armband. The cloth felt heavy in her palm—too heavy for its size. "When?"

"Tomorrow night," Claire said. "The post changes shift then. They'll expect deliveries. If you can plant the explosives in their generator room, you'll cripple their signal for weeks."

Lukas looked at her, jaw tight. "And what if we refuse?"

Claire's gaze didn't soften. "Then you can keep running. The patrols will catch you before the week is out. Or you can do this and give yourselves a chance worth dying for."

Anna stared down at the map. Her reflection wavered in a small pool of spilled coffee, ghostlike. She thought of the letter that had destroyed her family, the people lost since. If they ran again, what would it mean? Another hiding place, another escape—but no end.

She met Lukas's eyes. "If we do this, maybe it ends something. For once."

He held her gaze, then nodded slowly. "All right," he said to Claire. "We'll do it."

Claire exhaled, the faintest relief breaking through her steel. "Good. Then eat. Rest. I'll have uniforms prepared. And pray the weather holds—rain makes the roads harder to patrol."

* * *

Later, when Claire left to speak with the others, Anna and Lukas remained at the table, staring at the map. Outside, the wind had picked up again, rattling the shutters.

Anna traced a finger along the red mark where the transmitter stood. "It's madness," she whispered.

Lukas gave a low laugh, almost tender. "Everything we've done since the trenches has been madness."

She looked at him, and in his tired smile she saw both fear and something stronger—the same stubborn defiance that had kept them alive.

"Then we'll go together," she said.

"Always," he answered.

Outside, dawn brightened the horizon—a thin, uncertain light breaking through the gray clouds. It fell across the map like a promise and a warning both, glinting off the red cross still clenched in Anna's trembling hand.

Tomorrow night, they would walk straight into the lion's den.

And this time, there would be no running left.

CHAPTER TWENTY-ONE:
Under the Flag of Iron

The night lay heavy over Charleville — the kind of black that swallowed sound and breath alike. The German flag above the depot flapped wetly in the wind, crimson catching the glint of searchlights. Beyond the wire fence, rows of trucks and tents blurred into shadow. Somewhere inside the main building, the transmitter pulsed — a rhythmic signal that meant death for every resistance cell it touched.

Anna adjusted her Red Cross armband, the fabric stiff with rain. "You remember the plan?" she whispered.

Lukas, pale beneath his helmet, nodded once. His left arm was bandaged to the shoulder, his tunic torn to look like shrapnel had found him. Beneath the wrappings lay the compact explosive Claire Duret had given them — disguised as a morphine pump. "Walk straight, look hurt," he murmured with a wry half-smile. "Easy enough."

They moved toward the gate. A sentry called out — "Halt! Identify yourselves!" — and Lukas staggered forward, letting his limp speak before his voice did.

"Private Hans Rainer. Wounded at the rail junction. Medical evacuation order." He swayed, teeth clenched as if in pain. Anna rushed to steady him, pressing a hand to his chest.

"He's losing blood," she said quickly. "Field Command authorized transfer. Do you want him dying on your steps?"

The guard hesitated, then waved them through. "The infirmary's to the left. Be quick about it."

Inside the depot, heat and diesel thickened the air. Floodlights cast long shadows through the corridors; boots clattered against stone floors. Anna led Lukas down the main hall, nodding curtly to passing medics. To anyone looking, she was just another weary nurse escorting a casualty from the front.

They passed a doorway marked *Funkraum* – Radio Operations. The low hum of static reached her ears — the sound of coded German orders filling the airwaves.

Lukas's eyes met hers. *That's it.*

"Wait here," Anna said aloud for the benefit of a nearby orderly. "I'll find the attending physician."

When the man turned away, Lukas ducked into the radio room. A sergeant sat at the desk, headphones on, jotting signals into a ledger. Lukas's hand shot out — the butt of his pistol struck clean and hard. The man slumped silently.

Anna slipped in behind him, pulling the door closed. The transmitter loomed against the far wall — massive, humming, its dials glowing like small suns.

"Set it beneath the console," she whispered.

Lukas knelt, unwrapping the bandage to reveal the compact charge. His fingers worked quickly, threading the fuse through the wires. Anna stood watch, pulse hammering as footsteps echoed somewhere beyond the door.

A voice barked, "Sergeant! Report!"

Anna grabbed a clipboard, thrust open the door, and barked in turn, "He's treating a field casualty. Orders from Captain Reinhard!"

The officer blinked, muttered something, and moved on. Anna closed the door and exhaled. "Two minutes."

Lukas struck the detonator. A faint whine rose as the timer engaged. "Time to go."

They slipped back into the corridor. Lukas leaned on her arm, feigning collapse, his weight nearly real — he'd reopened the gash on his leg climbing the fence earlier. They passed the gate just as thunder cracked — or what sounded like thunder.

A second later, the ground trembled.

Flame burst from the depot's far windows, licking skyward, shards of glass raining onto the mud. Sirens screamed. Soldiers shouted orders, racing toward the blaze. Anna and Lukas stumbled along the outer road, vanishing into the confusion.

In the distance, the radio tower folded in on itself, its iron spine glowing red before it fell. The transmitter — the lifeline of Command — was gone.

Lukas gritted his teeth, clutching his side. "That's one for the resistance."

Anna tightened her hold on him, guiding him toward the shadows of the treeline. "And one step closer to saving my parents."

Behind them, the depot burned — and for the first time in weeks, the coded German signals fell silent across the air.

* * *

The road to the safe house wound through rain-soaked fields and stands of pine, their needles whispering in the wind. By the time Anna and Lukas reached the farmhouse, dawn had begun to smudge the eastern horizon in bruised pink. Smoke from the destroyed depot still smeared the sky behind them.

A hand signal from the hedgerow brought the wooden door open a crack. "Passphrase?"

"Edelweiss," Anna rasped.

The door swung wide. Claire Duret stood there, her cloak streaked with mud, eyes sharp as bayonets. "Inside, quickly."

They ducked through into the dim interior. The safe house smelled of lamp oil and damp wool. A map of the Ardennes was tacked to the wall beside a battered radio that now gave only static. Around the table sat three other resistance members: Étienne, the railway man; Margot, the courier; and a young Belgian boy barely sixteen who handled their code relays.

Anna helped Lukas to a chair. He winced as he sat, clutching the bandaged leg.
Claire crouched beside him, inspecting the wound with practiced hands. "You made it out," she said. "We saw the fire from the ridge."

Lukas nodded faintly. "The transmitter's gone. Nothing left but twisted steel."

Margot let out a low whistle. "Then it worked."

But Étienne's expression was grim. He tapped the radio casing. "A message came through before the lines went dead. The blast spread to the supply depot next door. Two dozen soldiers were killed. Three civilian workers, too."

Silence fell, thick and choking. The sound of rain on the shutters filled the space.

186

Anna's hands trembled. "Civilians? There weren't supposed to be—"

"They were forced labor," Claire said quietly. "Mostly locals. The Gestapo will blame partisans. They've already set up roadblocks from Sedan to Reims."

Lukas lowered his gaze, jaw tightening. "So our victory buys us another round of reprisals."

Claire met his eyes. "Yes. But it also buys us silence. Command can't track our couriers now, or your parents."

Anna looked up sharply. "You found them?"

Claire hesitated, then nodded toward a folded sheet on the table. "Intercepted orders from Charleville before the explosion. Transfer of prisoners Abraham and Miriam Müller cancelled—'lost contact with transmitter; hold for reassignment. 'They're alive, Anna. But they'll move them soon, likely to Mainz."

Relief and dread collided in her chest. She gripped the edge of the table until her knuckles whitened. "We have to go after them."

"We will," Lukas said, his voice low, steady. "But first, you need rest. We both do."

Anna shook her head. "Every hour we wait—"

"—Is another hour the roads are crawling with patrols?" Claire interrupted. "You've lit up half the Western Front tonight. Let them search ghosts while we plan the next move."

She poured coffee into tin cups, passing one to Anna. The bitter heat steadied her hands a little. Lukas leaned back, exhaustion carving shadows beneath his eyes. For the first time since the explosion, she let herself truly look at him—mud-streaked, blood-spattered, but alive.

"We did what we had to," he said quietly, more to himself than to her.

Anna met his gaze. "And we'll do it again. But next time, no innocents."

He reached across the table, his fingers brushing hers. "Next time, we find your parents."

Outside, the rain began again—soft, persistent, washing the last embers of the burning depot into the earth. In the flicker of the single lamp, the resistance planned their next move, knowing the cost of silence had only just begun.

* * *

The storm had been building all day, pressing against the shutters until the hinges rattled. Anna sat near the hearth, wiping sweat from Lukas's forehead. His fever had broken hours ago, but the trembling hadn't stopped; each breath caught against his ribs, shallow and uncertain.

A sudden pounding rattled the door. Claire rose, her hand instinctively going to the pistol lying beside the stove. She crossed the room soundlessly.

Lukas tensed in his chair, his face tightening.

"Stay still," Anna whispered.

The knock came again—three quick raps, a pause, then two more. Her heart jumped. That was the signal.

Claire hurried to the door and unlatched it.

Anna's pulse jumped. The door creaked open, and wind burst through, carrying rain and the smell of mud. Two figures filled the threshold, dripping wet and hollow-eyed. Two mud-streaked figures filled the threshold—Matthias and Erich, their faces gaunt but grinning, breath steaming in the cold.

"Matthias?" Lukas's voice was a rasp, disbelieving.

Matthias froze as if seeing a ghost. "*Gott im Himmel,*" Matthias laughed, grabbing Lukas's shoulders before he could speak. "We thought you were dead!"

Erich pushed past him, half laughing, half choking on the sound. "God—Lukas! You're alive!"

Lukas's eyes widened. "Matthias? Erich?" His voice cracked with joy on their names. "How—?" He could barely breathe.

Erich stepped forward, removing his cap, his blond hair matted, and his uniform torn. "The blast threw us clear. We crawled through a drainage ditch and followed the smoke east until we found the others." He smiled—tired, but real. "You look like you've been through hell."

"You bastard—you're alive!" Matthias grinned. "You fool! We buried you in our heads a dozen times!"

Lukas managed a crooked smile. "You sound disappointed."

"*Verdammt!* I've never been happier to be wrong." Matthias clasped his friend's shoulder carefully, mindful of the bandaged thigh. "We thought we'd lost you in the fire."

Before anyone could speak again, Lukas tried to stand. His leg buckled, and Matthias caught him by the shoulders, holding him upright the way he had in the trenches. The contact said everything words could not express.

Anna stepped back, watching them—these men bound by war, by loss, now whole for a fleeting instant. Even in the storm's roar, she heard the uneven sound of their breaths, the quiet disbelief that they were all still here.

"What happened after the train?" Lukas asked.

Matthias's jaw tightened. "We ran. Hid in the culverts. Thought you were gone."

Erich hovered near Lukas's chair, his usual reserve breaking into open warmth. "You were half buried under debris when we last saw you. How did you get out?"

Anna smiled faintly. *"Die Krankenträger*. He refused to die."

Lukas reached for her hand, his fingers brushing hers. "Friends, meet Anna. Anna, this is Matthias, and this is Erich."

Matthias barked a laugh. *"Du alter Hund!"* (You old son of a gun) and slapped him on the back.

But there's a network now—stronger than anything we had before. We've been waiting for a chance to finish what we started."

Erich managed a tired grin. "Looks like that chance found us again."

Lukas's eyes flicked to Anna, then back to them. "Then we finish it together."

Rain thundered against the windows, but inside, for the first time in weeks, the air felt warmer.

The small room filled with their laughter—rough, incredulous, edged with the relief of the living. For a moment, it didn't feel like war at all.

Erich rummaged in his satchel and pulled out a wrapped bundle. "We brought what we could." He opened it to reveal a heel of dark bread, a tin of sardines, and a flask. "Not much, but it's better than starving."

Claire's eyes shone. "You're a saint."

"Hardly," Erich muttered, handing the bread to Lukas first.

They sat together near the hearth, steam rising from their damp coats, the sound of rain soft against the shutters. Lukas ate slowly, wincing as he moved, but color had already begun to return to his face.

It was Matthias who spoke first. "When the train went up," he said, voice low, "I thought we were finished. The whole sky turned white. You were nearest the cars—I saw you go down. Erich dragged me behind the embankment before the second blast."

Erich gave a grim half-smile. "I told him you were gone, Lukas. There was nothing left but fire and metal."

Matthias stared into the flames. "We crawled into the culvert under the track. The air down there was poison—smoke, oil, blood. We stayed two days, waiting for the patrols to pass." He rubbed a hand over his face. "When we came out, they were collecting bodies. We almost joined them."

Erich leaned forward. "We followed the drainage ditch west. Found a bakery still standing. The woman there—Frau Lenz—hid us in her cellar. She worked with the Resistance. Radioed someone in Darmstadt who knew how to get deserters out."

Matthias's mouth tightened. "We didn't mean to join them. At first, we just wanted to survive. But then we saw what they did with the story—they blamed the explosion on Jews and civilians. Said *traitors* destroyed their own train. My brother's name was on the list of 'accomplices. 'They executed him the next morning."

He paused, swallowing hard. "That's when I stopped being a soldier."

The room was silent but for the rain. Lukas's throat ached. "You could have run," he said quietly. "Crossed the border. Started over."

Erich shook his head. "Liesel would've wanted me to fight. You remember her? Handing out those leaflets about truth and freedom? They took her for it. I still don't know where." His eyes glinted in the firelight. "If the Resistance could hurt the bastards who did that—then that's where I belonged."

Matthias looked up at Lukas. "And you? You're still fighting, even half-dead and hunted. Maybe we were always meant to meet again."

Lukas tried to smile, though pain flickered through it. "Maybe God thought three ghosts would do better than one."

Erich laughed under his breath, the sound shaky but real. "Then let's make it count this time."

Outside, thunder rolled across the river valley. Inside, the three men sat together again—no longer soldiers under orders, but brothers who had chosen the same war for their own reasons.

Matthias leaned back against the wall, watching Lukas. "You always were too stubborn to die."

Lukas smiled faintly. "And you always turn up when I least expect it."

"Then we'll keep doing that," Matthias said. "The three of us—like before."

For the first time in days, warmth filled the safe house—not from the fire, but from laughter, shared breath, the miracle of reunion.

Anna sat quietly beside Lukas, her hand resting over his. The men talked in low voices, planning, remembering, teasing—soldiers again, if only for a heartbeat.

The war would press in soon enough, the mission to Mainz waiting like a shadow on the map. But for now, as dawn brightened the room, they were simply friends who had found each other again in a world determined to take everything.

CHAPTER TWENTY-TWO:
The Road to Mainz

The room smelled of boiled cabbage and lamp oil. Lukas sat half-propped on a tattered settee, a wool blanket over his lap. His fever had returned. Anna sat at his feet, one hand curled around his wrist, listening.

Matthias shut the door behind him and leaned against it, shoulders hunched as if the news had pressed into his spine. Erich came in behind him, winded, a smear of mud on his sleeve, and that particular look of a man who'd run too far with hope and come back with only part of it.

"We weren't supposed to be seen," Matthias said without preamble. "We were supposed to take a quick look at the depot and come home. But we saw them moving—more than we expected."

Anna's throat tightened. She had learned, in the last days, the dangerous currency of words: a single sentence could buy a life or cost it. She kept her voice steady. "What did you see?"

Erich unrolled a scrap of paper—inks and creases, something stolen from an officer's pocket or slipped through a laundress's hand. He smoothed it on the table but didn't read it aloud. Instead, his eyes caught Anna's, and he let the quiet fill before he spoke.

"They're consolidating prisoners from the front into a single transfer," he said. "Mainz is the hub. They move them in groups to make accounting easier before shipping them farther inland. The resistance in the city intercepted word: a transfer is scheduled in the next two nights."

Lukas made a small sound and tightened his fingers around Anna's wrist; she squeezed back, grounding him. "Two nights?" she echoed. It felt like a countdown someone had lit and set on the edge of the world.

Matthias rubbed his forehead. "We don't know the exact hour — they're careful — but we do know the route. The guards will be heavier at the rail yard; lighter on the road into the city. There's a window when they move prisoners from the wagons to the holding pens. That's where they're exposed. A dozen men could mean the difference."

Anna felt the room tilt. For a heartbeat, she saw visions: rows of faces in dim wagons, the muffled sobs, the clinking of chains. Her fingers found Lukas's pulse again. "Who is among them?" she asked, voice thin.

Erich swallowed. "Mostly conscripts and men rounded after the last sweep. But —" he looked away for a beat, "— there's a name we heard. A lieutenant from the other side's intelligence—he's being moved for interrogation. If he talks, it could break more than one chain."

The words landed heavy, as if the room had been waiting for them. Anna's mind flashed to her parents: their dispatches, the risks they'd taken. Had those words in a letter funneled like water into these train cars? Guilt pricked her, sharp and useless. She forced the question into speech. "Could any of the prisoners be civilians? Families?"

"Some," Matthias said bluntly. "There are always civilians. The thing is, Anna — we can't ignore this. If they're taking people to Mainz to be sorted and shipped out, we can intercept before they vanish into the system. We can get them out of immediate danger."

195

Lukas 'brow creased in a way that made Anna's heart ache. He tried to speak, voice thin as linen. "You… don't have to tell me. I'm useless right now. Don't—" He stopped, because he did not want to be the reason they stayed.

Anna placed her palm over his lips, soft but certain. "Stop," she said. "You are not useless. Not to me. But listen," she turned to Matthias, "Tell me what you would need of me."

Matthias looked at her then, really looked, and something like respect and apology passed over his face. "We need someone who can handle what comes after — bandaging, tending, talking to men who've lost everything. If any of them get hurt in an attempt, they'll die without care. They'll need a steady hand. You're the best of us for that, Anna."

Erich leaned forward. "We have a contact in Mainz — a baker named Ernst. He owes us a favor. He can get a small safe room for a few hours, hide people long enough for us to move them out of the city. But he can't do it alone. We need a diversion that draws most of the guard detail away from the transfer point. Then someone — a few of us — make a run at the wagons while others shepherd the freed into Ernst's cellar."

Anna's breath caught. She had heard plans like this all her life from whispered mouths in kitchens; she had nursed men torn and broken by attempts that had missed. She had also felt the sickening knowledge that plans that sounded noble on paper could shred into rubble against a single unforeseen guard or a single misread signal.

"Divert," she repeated. The word tasted like ash. "How many would that take? How many people will you ask to risk themselves?"

Matthias 'jaw tightened. "More than we'd like to admit. Less than we have."

A silence folded over them. Lukas opened his eyes. "Anna," he said, like the name of a prayer. "If you go—if you go, promise me you'll be careful."

She looked at him, at the shadows under his eyes, and felt the double pull of duty: to the man who had given her his whole frightened heart and to the stranger whose life might hinge on a single choice. "I can't promise I'll be safe," she said honestly. "But I promise I'll do what I can to bring people back."

Matthias nodded once. "That's all any of us can ask. We'll take the risks we must. We'll try to keep it clean — a quick in-and-out. No lingering, no unnecessary bloodshed. We do what we can for the people we can save."

Erich tapped the paper on the table. "We leave at dusk. Ernst will have the cellar ready by nightfall. If we move too early, we'll be watched. Too late, and the prisoners will be gone. We have two nights 'window—if we fail the first, we try again the second. But after that, the schedule gets unpredictable."

Anna closed her eyes for a moment and imagined the faces she had treated these past weeks—boys who looked like her cousins, fathers who had wept for a life never given. She pictured the cramped wagons, the metallic taste of fear. She wanted, with a physical ache, to take their place.

"Then it's settled," she said, and when she spoke there was steel beneath the softness. "I'll come. I'll be with Ernst. I'll tend anyone who needs me. And when you fetch them, you'll bring them here if you can. We have to move before the army buries their tracks."

Matthias let out a breath he'd been holding. "We'll need a small team for the wagons. I'll take Erich and two others. Lukas—" He glanced toward the settee, and the decision hung there, gentle and cruel. "You rest. You heal. You'll come when you can."

Lukas managed a crooked laugh. "You're laying orders on me from a chair. Typical."

Anna kissed his brow then, without ceremony. It was a small heat against his clammy skin — a tether. "When this is done," she whispered, "we'll have a feast."

"That's right!" Matthias agreed. "Bread! Goose! Wine!"

Erich smiled, though his eyes stayed hard. "Then we'd better bring back a lot of people."

Outside, the wind thinned, riffling loose shutters. The idea of Mainz sat between them now like a living thing— vulnerable, urgent, hungry. They set about the quiet work of planning in gestures: Matthias checking the worn map tucked in his pocket, Erich going to fetch a blanket for Lukas, Anna making a list of supplies she would need to bandage, to calm, to stitch.

None of them spoke of the cost if it failed. You didn't say those things out loud in a room where had to sleep. But whenever their hands brushed over the lamp-blackened table, each knew the measure of what they were asking of one another.

They had two nights. They had a contact and a sliver of intelligence. And they had each other—flawed, frightened, and determined as ever.

When dusk came, the plan would have to be tested against real noise and real fear. For now, in the oil-light of the safe house, they prepared the smallest of rebellions: the hope that they could pull a ragged handful of souls back from the jaws of a system that would chew them up and forget their names.

* * *

The streets of Mainz were slick with evening rain, the kind that turned dust into mud and made the gaslights blur at their edges. A soft steam rose from the bakery on the corner of Holzstraße, where Ernst Becker worked through the night, kneading dough with arms like oak and nerves that hadn't settled in years.

He'd left the front long ago—one leg shortened by a shell fragment—but the war had a way of finding every man, even those who thought they'd escaped it. Tonight, it waited for him in the creak of the shutters, in the hiss of the oven, in the muffled beat of boots he could hear even through the steady rhythm of rain.

He glanced toward the cellar door—half-hidden behind stacked flour sacks. Beneath it, a single lantern burned, dim and steady. The place smelled of yeast and damp stone. He'd swept the floor, cleared the barrels, even laid out an old blanket or two.

They said only a few, he thought grimly. *A few souls, in and out, quiet as smoke.*

He wasn't sure he believed in quiet anymore.

The bell above the front door jingled, sharp and out of place. Ernst froze, flour dust clinging to his arms like frost. He wiped his hands on his apron and stepped into the shop.

Two figures stood there—coats soaked, caps pulled low. The taller one had a bandage on his forearm, the smaller one carried a folded map tucked inside her coat.

"Evening," Ernst said softly. "You're early."

Matthias nodded once, pulling the cap lower. "We had to move sooner. Patrols are heavier near the yard."

Behind him, Anna stepped into the light. Her cheeks were pale, her eyes fierce and hollow from sleeplessness. She carried a satchel of bandages slung across her shoulder like a soldier's pack.

"Is the cellar ready?" she asked.

Ernst gestured toward the back. "As ready as it can be. You'll want the far corner—it's dry. No light unless you need it. I can bake long enough to mask the noise if it comes."

She gave him a weary smile. "*Danke*, Ernst. You could have said no."

He shrugged, looking away. "I've seen what happens when no one says yes."

From the alley, a low whistle—their signal. Erich slipped through the back, dripping and wide-eyed. "They've begun loading. Two wagons are already at the yard gate. We've got maybe twenty minutes before they move."

Matthias leaned over the flour-dusted counter, spreading the small, rain-wrinkled map. "Here. The rail spur runs east to the river. They'll take the prisoners through here"—his finger traced a narrow lane—"then down to the bridge. That's our choke point. Erich, you and I draw them off near the brewery. The rest move in from the south wall."

"And me?" Anna asked.

"You stay here. If we're lucky, we'll send a handful back with you. If not…" He let the silence finish the thought.

Anna pressed her lips together, then nodded. She understood. In war, luck was the only thing that ever truly arrived on time.

Erich tightened his gloves. "We'll start the diversion in ten."

They slipped out into the rain. The bell above the door jingled once more, then silence swallowed it. The night swallowed them whole.

Mainz crouched low under a blanket of mist—rows of shuttered houses, a few stray dogs, the far-off glow of the rail yard like a furnace's eye. The air reeked faintly of coal smoke and wet bread from Ernst's ovens, a scent that mingled with the metallic taste of fear.

At the corner near the brewery, Matthias lifted his hand. "Here," he whispered. "You see them?"

Through the fog, the column appeared—guards with rifles slung over their shoulders, prisoners shuffling in mud, the chains between them glinting faintly in the lamplight. The sound—boots, chains, coughs—was too human, too close.

Erich exhaled slowly. "There's more than a dozen."

Matthias nodded. "Then we'll have to be clever."

He pulled a small satchel from his coat and crouched by the drain. A thin thread of smoke curled up as he lit the fuse. The flare would burst two streets away—a distraction, loud enough to scatter the guard patrols but not close enough to kill.

"Run when it blows," he said. "I'll be right behind."

* * *

Ernst could feel it before he heard it—the low rumble that rolled through the cobblestones like a drumbeat. Flour sifted down from the ceiling. The windowpanes rattled.

Anna's hand went to her satchel. "That's them," she murmured.

A moment later, the back door banged open. Two men half-dragged, half-carried a prisoner through mud-caked, dazed, one arm bleeding freely. Another stumbled in behind them, coughing.

"Get them below!" one of the men hissed. "Quickly!"

Anna guided them toward the cellar. "This way. Down the steps."

The wounded man collapsed at her feet, whispering something she couldn't catch. His sleeve bore the insignia of a French regiment. She pressed a hand to his shoulder. "You're safe now," she said in halting French. "Stay quiet. Breathe."

Ernst hurried to bolt the door behind them, his hands shaking. "How many?"

"More coming," one of the resistance men gasped. "Matthias and Erich are still out there—they drew most of the guards east, but they won't hold long."

Anna tore a strip of cloth with her teeth and wrapped the Frenchman's arm. "We'll hold until dawn if we must," she said. "Just keep that door closed."

The cellar filled slowly—five, then ten souls—each dripping, trembling, eyes wide with disbelief at safety. Ernst passed around loaves from the cooling rack above, the smell of crust and yeast filling the damp air.

Upstairs, the bakery's oven crackled. It was the only sound that masked the noise of frightened breathing below.

Hours passed in fragments: footsteps above, then silence; a shout in the street, then wind. Anna worked until her hands cramped—cleaning wounds, whispering comfort.

When at last the back door opened again, Matthias stumbled in, mud to his knees, smoke on his face. Erich followed, limping, his sleeve burned.

"Did you—?" Ernst began.

Matthias nodded, breathless. "We got them. Not all, but enough. The others scattered. They'll make for the woods by morning."

Anna reached for him, steadying his shoulder. "And Lukas?" she asked before she could stop herself.

Matthias 'expression softened. "Alive. He'll curse us for leaving him behind, but he'll live."

Anna laughed then—short, wet, half a sob—and wiped her cheek with the back of her hand.

Ernst poured what was left of his wine into tin cups and passed them around. "For those who made it," he said quietly, "and for those who will."

They drank in silence.

Outside, the rain eased. Somewhere in the distance, a clock tolled three. The city of Mainz slept on, unaware that beneath one small bakery, the course of a dozen lives had just shifted—saved not by armies or orders, but by hands that refused to stay idle while others suffered.

CHAPTER TWENTY-THREE:
After the Interception

By morning, the rain had stopped, leaving the streets slick and silver. A pale mist clung to the rooftops, and from the bakery chimney, the first smoke of the day rose as if nothing extraordinary had happened at all.

Down in the cellar, the air was thick with the scent of sweat, bread, and wet wool. Anna had not slept. She sat on a crate beside the wounded Frenchman, checking his pulse with trembling fingers. Around her, a dozen men and one woman huddled in the dim light—faces hollowed by hunger and fear, but alive.

Ernst came down the steps carrying a fresh loaf and a tin of water. "They're stirring," he said softly. "The city's quiet so far. No patrols near Holzstraße. But that won't last."

Anna looked up at him, her voice rasped thin. "How long before they notice the missing men?"

Ernst shrugged. "By noon, maybe. The guards will say fog delayed them, then they'll start counting. You have until then."

Anna moved among the rescued like a shadow—quiet, careful, her eyes searching every face. Bandages were being changed, bread divided, and water poured into tin cups. The soft murmurs of gratitude blended with the low moans of the wounded.

But she wasn't listening anymore. Her pulse hammered in her ears.

She paused by the Frenchman, his arm now tightly wrapped in linen. "Merci," he whispered, voice barely audible. She smiled, nodded, but her gaze was already moving on—to the next man, then the next. A farmer from Alsace. A tailor from Metz. A boy from Koblenz.

None of them were her parents.

Her stomach twisted. *Please, Elohim, just one sign. One word.*

She turned to Matthias, who was crouched near the door, checking his revolver with steady hands that didn't match the exhaustion in his eyes.

"Matthias," she said. Her voice trembled, and she steadied it before she spoke again. "You said there were civilians among the prisoners. Did anyone—did anyone mention names?"

He looked up, the kind of look that came from a man who already knew where this was going. "Whose names?"

"My parents," she said. "Abraham and Miriam Müller. They were taken in the last sweep near Koblenz. I thought— maybe..." She trailed off, eyes darting toward the huddled figures. "If the transport came through here, they might have been among them."

Matthias exhaled slowly, his breath fogging in the chill. He rose and crossed to her, his boots crunching softly on the grit of the floor. "Anna," he began carefully, "we asked the ones who could still speak. No one's heard those names."

Her face fell. "You're sure?"

"I'm sure they weren't on the wagons we hit." He hesitated, lowering his voice. "There are… other routes. Some go farther east. Some never pass through Mainz at all."

Anna's throat tightened. "Then we were too late."

"Not necessarily," he said gently. "There are still transports coming. We'll keep listening. You know the resistance passes messages through the camps. If your parents are alive, word will reach us."

She nodded numbly, but her eyes didn't leave the rescued crowd. One of the women—a frail figure in a torn shawl—was being given a sip of water by Ernst. For a fleeting moment, Anna's breath caught; the woman's profile in the lantern light looked achingly familiar.

Anna stepped forward. "Entschuldigen Sie—please—your name?"

The woman blinked at her, startled. "Elsa," she whispered, voice hoarse. "Elsa Hoffmann."

Anna's shoulders sagged. She forced a smile. "You're safe now, Elsa. Rest."

She turned back to Matthias, her composure cracking. "If they were on a different route—if they were sent east—then we may never—"

He cut her off, laying a hand on her arm. "No. Don't think like that. We're still here, and so are they until we know otherwise. Your parents helped half the people in this room with their dispatches. This"—he gestured at the cellar, at the living proof of it—"is their work as much as ours."

Anna looked around the room again—at the wounded boy asleep under a blanket, at the men who still trembled from hunger, at the faint rise and fall of their chests. She wanted to believe him.

But all she could think of was her mother's gentle hands at the kitchen table, her father's careful voice murmuring codes beneath the candlelight.

"Then we'll find them," she said quietly, more to herself than anyone. "We have to."

Matthias nodded once. "We will."

The cellar door creaked above them—Ernst's signal. Morning patrols were sweeping the neighborhood. Matthias turned toward the steps, his tone snapping back to command. "Everyone ready. We move before the hour turns."

Anna took one last look at the faces in the room—the living, the nearly dead, the terrified—and whispered a prayer that somewhere out there, two more faces still waited to be found.

Then she followed Matthias up into the light.

Matthias, sitting near the wall, ran a hand over his unshaven face. His coat was still damp, and his knuckles were raw. "We can't move them all," he said finally. "Half of them can barely stand."

Erich crouched by the door, watching the slit of light at the bottom. "Hans can get a wagon—maybe two seats under flour sacks. But that's for the worst of them only. The rest will have to walk out with us by nightfall."

Anna pressed her palms together, trying to still the trembling. "And where will you take them?"

"There's a farm north of here," Matthias said. "A safe stop. If we get them there, they can disperse. But we can't draw too much attention on the road. A large group will be caught within an hour."

The Frenchman stirred, murmuring weakly. Anna bent close, catching fragments in his language. "He says one of the others can't walk," she translated softly. "A leg wound. He says they'll stay behind if they must."

Matthias shook his head. "No one stays behind in the open. Ernst?"

The baker rubbed the back of his neck, eyes darting toward the ceiling as if weighing invisible scales. "There's the old coal storage under the oven. My father built it before the war. No one's used it in years—it's hidden behind the old stones. Two, maybe three people could fit, if they don't mind the dark."

Anna's gaze flicked to the weakest among them—a boy who couldn't be more than seventeen, his arm bandaged tight against his chest, and a thin man who coughed blood into his sleeve. She knew the answer before anyone spoke.

"Those two," she said quietly. "They stay here. The rest will move tonight."

Matthias looked at her, pain in his eyes. "If they're found—"

"They won't be," she interrupted. "Ernst will keep the oven hot. The soldiers won't linger near a working hearth. It's the safest place left."

Ernst nodded once, grim but resolute. "Then that's what we'll do."

For a moment, no one spoke. The silence felt heavier than the stones above them. Then Matthias rose and touched Anna's shoulder. "You should go back soon," he said gently. "Lukas—he'll want to see you. He woke sometime after dawn."

She froze. "He's awake?"

Matthias nodded. "Claire's keeping him still, but he's asking questions."

A breath of relief escaped her before she could stop it. Her eyes stung. "Then I'll go. But not until they're settled."

* * *

When Anna finally returned, the sky had cleared to a pale, cold blue. The streets between Mainz and the outskirts were washed clean by the night's rain, though the stench of smoke and fear still clung to the air.

The safe house door creaked as she slipped inside. Lukas was awake—sitting propped on pillows, a blanket wrapped around his shoulders. His face was still pale, but color was returning to his lips. When he saw her, his expression shifted from relief to anger and back again, as though he couldn't decide which feeling would win.

"You went," he said hoarsely. "You went without me."

Anna stood in the doorway, mud on her boots, her braid coming loose. "You were half-conscious," she answered softly. "You couldn't even stand."

"You could have waited—"

"Waited while men were loaded onto wagons like cattle?" Her voice trembled, the fatigue cracking through. "While women were taken to God knows where? No, Lukas. We had a chance, and we took it."

He looked away, jaw tightening. "Matthias told me enough. You risked everything. If they'd caught you—"

"They didn't." She crossed the room, lowering herself beside him. "And I'd do it again."

For a long moment they sat in silence. The only sound was the faint hum of morning through cracked windows—the world going on, as if unaware that it had almost ended for a few dozen souls beneath a bakery.

Lukas finally turned to her, eyes dark with something that wasn't anger anymore. "How many?" he asked quietly.

"Twelve made it," she said. "Two stayed behind with Ernst. They're hidden until they're strong enough to move."

He nodded slowly, rubbing a hand over his face. "You saved them."

"We saved them," she corrected. "All of us."

He looked at her then—really looked. "You shouldn't have to bear this."

She smiled faintly. "Neither should you."

Her hand brushed his as she reached to adjust the blanket. He caught it halfway, his grip weak but insistent. "Anna… promise me something."

"What?"

"That when this is over—if it ever ends—you'll let yourself rest. That you'll stop running toward the fire."

Her throat tightened. "Only if you promise the same."

He gave a weary, crooked smile. "Then I can't promise."

She leaned in, pressing her forehead lightly against his. "Nor can I."

Outside, the church bells began to toll—a sound deep and resonant, cutting through the hush of the waking city. Each chime seemed to mark something new: survival, loss, and the fragile defiance of still being alive.

Matthias 'shadow appeared briefly in the doorway, his voice low. "The wagons are ready. We move the others tonight."

Anna didn't look up. She only whispered, "Then we start again."

* * *

The lamp burned low, its weak flame trembling each time the wind pressed against the shutters. Anna sat on the edge of the cot, her sleeves rolled past her elbows, hands steady though her heart raced beneath her uniform.

Lukas stirred, the fever still holding him. His skin was slick with sweat, his breath shallow. She wrung out the cloth in the basin beside her, the water now cloudy from herbs and sweat, and pressed it gently to his brow.

"Shh…" she whispered. "It's all right."

He opened his eyes halfway—gray and distant. "Anna?"

"I'm here." Her voice softened, though inside she was breaking. "You have to rest. The fever will break soon."

He tried to shift, but the pain caught him, a low groan escaping his lips. She placed a hand against his chest, firm but gentle. "Don't move. You'll tear the stitches. Again."

The wound in his thigh was angry and red, though the edges had begun to knit beneath the bandage. She peeled it back carefully, the smell of antiseptic sharp in the chill air. She had boiled what little water they had left, mixed it with the last of her tinctures, and prayed it would be enough.

Outside, the world was silent except for distant guns—muffled thunder rolling across the front. They were supposed to leave by dawn, to reach the safe house before the next patrols swept the road. But looking at Lukas now—so pale, trembling despite the blankets—Anna knew they would have to risk slowing down.

She dipped the cloth again, cooling his skin, murmuring to herself more than to him. "If you die on me now, I swear I'll never forgive you."

His lips twitched, the ghost of a smile. "Bossy… nurse."

Her throat caught at the sound of his voice. "Someone has to keep you alive."

He blinked slowly, fighting the pull of sleep. "Then stay… with me."

"I can't," she said, brushing the damp hair from his forehead. "I have to find my parents. We have to move soon. Claire will watch over you. Can you stand, when the time comes?"

He didn't answer, just reached weakly for her hand. She took it, feeling the tremor in his fingers.

"Then I'll carry you if I must," she whispered, her eyes fierce now despite the tears. "We're getting out of this place together, Lukas Schneider. Do you hear me?"

The fever broke near dawn. When she touched his face again, the heat had eased. He slept at last—deeply, quietly—and Anna leaned over him, exhaustion flooding her bones. Outside, the first gray light crept over the broken fields. They would move soon.

But for one fragile hour, she let herself rest beside him, her head against his shoulder, listening to the steady beat of his heart.

CHAPTER TWENTY-FOUR:
Escape

The dawn never truly came, only a bruised gray light through the mist. Lukas was awake but weak, pale, and hollow-eyed. Anna had promised she would return before the sun was high, and she meant it.

"Stay hidden," she told him softly, fastening her cloak. "We'll be back before nightfall."

Lukas wanted to argue, but one look at her face silenced him. "Be careful," he murmured. "If you find them—"

"I will." She pressed his hand once, then slipped out into the fog.

* * *

The village lay in ruins when Anna, Erich, and Matthias crept along the back road, moving between the wrecked barns and burned wagons. The air still smelled of ash and cordite. Somewhere, a dog barked and was quickly silenced.

Matthias raised a hand, signaling for quiet. They crouched in the mud behind a low wall. Ahead, the cellar door of the old millhouse—the one the resistance had used before the last bombardment—was half-buried beneath fallen beams.

"That's where they hid," whispered Erich. "The others should still be below."

Anna's pulse quickened. "My parents?"

Matthias's eyes met hers. He nodded hopefully.

They waited until a patrol passed, boots squelching through the muck. Then they ran. The boards creaked beneath their feet, but the cellar door gave way under Matthias's crowbar with only a muted groan.

"Anna—go," he urged.

She slipped down the narrow steps first, the air growing damp and cold. The scent of earth and fear clung to the darkness.

"Hallo? Ernst?" she whispered. "Mama? Papa?"

For a long moment, there was only silence—then a rustle, a faint gasp.

"Anna?"

The voice broke her heart open. "Mama!" She stumbled forward, nearly tripping over a crate, and then arms were around her—thin, trembling arms, her mother's shawl rough against her cheek.

"Mein Kind," her mother sobbed, kissing her hair again and again. "We thought you were gone."

Behind her, a lantern flickered to life. Her father, pale but unbroken, stood beside the others— Ernst, three villagers, an old man, a wounded boy. He set down the lantern and crossed to her, gripping her shoulders.

"You came back for us." His voice was hoarse. "We heard the explosions—we thought—"

"We have to move now," Matthias interrupted gently, keeping his voice low. "There's a patrol sweeping this way within the hour."

Anna nodded, blinking tears away. "We've got a safe house beyond the ridge. Lukas is there—he's alive. We can get everyone out if we leave before sunrise."

Erich was already helping the old man to his feet, checking the boy's bandages. "There's a wagon behind the mill, half hidden. If we keep to the fields—"

Her father picked up his satchel. "Then let's go."

Anna squeezed her mother's hand, unwilling to let go even as they climbed the steps back into the gray dawn. For the first time in weeks, hope felt real—fragile, trembling, but alive.

As they reached the ridge and the wind carried the first echo of gunfire from the town behind them, Matthias turned to Anna. "We found them," he said quietly.

Anna looked back toward the smoking rooftops, then ahead toward the hills where Lukas waited. "Not all," she whispered, "but enough to keep fighting."

The fog thickened as they left the cellar behind, swallowing the broken outlines of the mill and the smoking ruins of the village. Every footstep sank into the sodden earth, each breath a pale ghost in the cold dawn.

Matthias led the way, his pistol drawn, his coat dark with mud. Erich brought up the rear with the old man slung across his shoulder and the boy limping beside him. Anna and her parents kept low between them, her mother's hand gripping hers so tightly it almost hurt.

"Stay close," Matthias murmured. "There's a patrol to the east—three men, maybe four. They've got dogs."

The word made Anna's heart clench. Dogs meant they were sweeping for survivors.

She pulled her scarf tighter around her face and crouched as they crossed the open field. The fog gave them cover, but every few steps came the jingle of distant metal, the muted bark of an order in German.

"Down," Matthias hissed, gesturing sharply.

They dropped into the ditch just as a column of soldiers passed on the road above them. Anna could see their boots through the reeds—heavy, caked with mud, the silver of bayonets glinting faintly in the gray. One of the men stopped, lighting a cigarette. The flare illuminated his face for a heartbeat—tired, young, oblivious to the fugitives lying not ten feet away.

Anna pressed her hand over her mother's trembling fingers, silently willing her to stay still. The smoke drifted downwind, sharp and acrid. For one terrible moment, the soldier turned his head, peering into the mist.

Then Matthias's hand touched her arm—*wait*—and slowly the sound of boots faded again, swallowed by the fog.

Only when they were gone did anyone dare to breathe.

Erich exhaled sharply. "Too close."

"Not close enough to stop us," Matthias muttered. "Move."

They followed a drainage gully toward the woods. Once under the cover of trees, the air smelled of pine and damp earth instead of smoke. Anna's father stumbled once, clutching his chest, but waved her off when she tried to help.

"I can manage," he said quietly. "We've come too far to slow down now."

From somewhere behind them came a sharp whistle. Then another answered, farther off.

"They've found the cellar," Erich said grimly.

"Run," Matthias ordered.

They broke into a half-run, half-stumble through the trees, the wounded boy leaning on Anna's shoulder, her mother gasping for breath. Branches tore at their clothes, and every step was agony, but no one stopped.

Gunfire cracked in the distance—one shot, then two. The echoes seemed to chase them through the forest.

"Keep to the ravine!" Matthias called. "It'll muffle our tracks!"

They slid down the slope into a shallow stream, icy water biting through their boots. Anna nearly fell, but her father caught her, his hand steady despite his shaking.

"Almost there," he said. "The ridge isn't far."

When at last they saw the low stone bridge and the crooked signpost marking the back road to the safe house, Matthias slowed, motioning for silence again. He crouched behind a boulder, scanning the path ahead.

"All clear," he said finally. "No movement."

They crossed one by one. The sun was just beginning to burn through the fog, turning it gold at the edges. By the time they reached the far side of the hill, the sound of pursuit had faded to nothing but memory.

Anna turned and looked back. The valley behind them was still, the smoke of the village curling faintly against the morning sky.

Her mother leaned against her shoulder. "We're safe now?"

Anna nodded, though her voice trembled. "For now."

Matthias met her eyes. "Let's get them to Lukas before dark."

And so they pressed on—seven figures moving through the broken hills, toward the one fragile light of safety left to them in a war that had taken everything but hope.

By the time they reached the farmhouse, dusk had begun to settle over the fields. The wind carried the smell of rain, and the first drops struck the roof as Matthias pushed the door open.

Inside, the single lamp flickered, casting long shadows across the walls. Lukas struggled to sit up from the cot the moment he heard them.

"Anna!" His voice cracked with relief.

She was at his side in an instant. "We made it back," she whispered, kneeling beside him. Her hands trembled as she brushed his hair back, tracing the familiar lines of his face. "We found them—my parents—they're here."

Claire came running from the kitchen to welcome them.

Lukas blinked, his eyes adjusting to the dim light as her mother and father stepped hesitantly into view. Her mother pressed a hand to her lips, tears spilling silently.

"Mein Gott," her father breathed. "You're alive."

Lukas tried to rise, wincing as his leg protested, but Anna stopped him. "No—don't. You're still healing."

Her mother came forward, her eyes glistening. "So this is the soldier who kept our daughter safe."

Lukas gave a faint, wry smile. "She's the one who kept *me* alive."

That earned a weak laugh from the room, the first sound of something like peace any of them had heard in weeks.

Erich eased the old man to the floor, rubbing his aching shoulders. "We can't stay long," he said, glancing toward the shuttered windows. "Patrols are combing the valley. It's only a matter of time before they reach the ridge."

Matthias nodded grimly. "He's right. We need to move by nightfall—before they close the road."

Anna's father frowned. "Move where? We've already lost half our people."

"There's another contact west of Mainz," Claire said. "An old brewery. The resistance uses it to move refugees and couriers through the line. If you reach it by dawn, you can get everyone across."

"What about you?" Erich said.

"Don't worry about me. I know how to handle myself," and she patted the gun at her side.

Anna turned to Lukas. "Can you travel?"

He exhaled slowly, pain shadowing his face. "If you help me."

"You shouldn't—"

"I can," he interrupted gently, his eyes steady on hers. "If we stay, they'll find us. You know that."

Her father looked between them. "Then it's settled."

Matthias began checking his revolver, sliding spare rounds into his coat pocket. "We leave when the rain's heaviest—it'll mask our tracks."

Anna's mother moved about the small kitchen, gathering what food remained: bread, two apples, a little cured meat. She wrapped them in cloth, pressing the bundle into Anna's hands. "You'll need strength," she said softly. "All of you."

Outside, thunder rolled. Lukas shifted, grimacing, and Anna steadied him. Their eyes met—his filled with stubborn resolve, hers with quiet fear.

"I told you I'd carry you if I had to," she murmured.

A faint smile tugged at his lips. "And I told you I'd walk beside you."

Matthias slung his pack over one shoulder. "Then let's go. The storm's here."

The group moved out into the rain, the farmhouse falling dark behind them. Anna glanced back once—the faint light in the window already swallowed by the night—and then forward again, toward the unknown.

Lukas leaned on her as they crossed the field, their footsteps lost in the downpour. Each drop felt like a heartbeat against her skin, a rhythm that meant one thing above all: they were still alive.

The storm came down like a wall, hard and relentless. The rain turned the track to black mire within minutes, soaking through their coats, plastering hair to skin. Every step was a battle against the sucking mud and the bitter wind.

Matthias moved at the front, lantern hooded, its thin beam cutting a narrow path through the darkness. Erich guided the old man and the boy behind him, while Anna and Lukas took the middle—her shoulder under his arm, his weight heavy but steady. Her parents followed, their outlines ghostlike in the rain.

Lightning split the sky ahead, illuminating the ruined farmland and the twisted shapes of abandoned wagons. The thunder that followed drowned all thought for a heartbeat.

Lukas stumbled, biting back a groan. Anna tightened her hold, her voice low and fierce. "One step at a time. We'll stop at the ridge."

"I'm fine," he managed, though the tremor in his voice betrayed him. "Just… promise me the road ahead is easier."

She gave a breathless laugh. "I can't even promise it's still there."

They trudged on. Each flash of light revealed more devastation—shattered trees, a cratered field, the skeleton of a farmhouse where someone had scrawled *Kein Zuhause mehr* (no more home) across a half-standing wall.

When they reached the ridge, Matthias motioned for them to stop beneath the cover of a collapsed barn. The rain drummed against the broken roof, dripping through the holes in slow, rhythmic beats.

"Rest here," he said quietly. "Ten minutes."

Anna helped Lukas lower himself to the ground. His leg was bleeding again; she tore a strip from her cloak and pressed it to the wound, her fingers numb.

"You should have stayed behind," she whispered.

"And miss all this?" he said faintly, nodding toward the storm. "Never."

She looked at him, rain tracing down her face. Even now, with his lips pale and his breath shallow, there was that same quiet determination—the one that had drawn her to him from the first.

Matthias crouched beside them, pulling a folded paper from his coat. "We got this from a contact in Frankfurt," he said, voice barely audible over the storm. "There's a prisoner transport scheduled through Mainz tomorrow night. They're moving someone important—someone the resistance's been trying to reach for months."

"Who?" Lukas asked, though his voice was weak.

"We don't know the name," Matthias said. "Only that Command wants him alive. A political prisoner. High-level, from Berlin, they think. He's being transferred through Mainz tonight under Gestapo escort."

Erich shook his head. "And we're supposed to do what? Wave a flag and ask nicely?"

Matthias ignored him. "There's an opportunity—just one. The truck convoy will stop at the rail yard for refueling. If we hit them there, we can get him out before dawn."

Anna, who had been quietly cleaning Lukas's wound, looked up sharply. "And you think it's worth risking everyone for a man we don't even know?"

Matthias's gaze met hers, steady and grim. "If Command wants him alive, he knows something worth dying for. And if the Gestapo wants him dead, that's reason enough to save him. If we can intercept the convoy, we'll have our chance to turn this war back in our favor."

Erich glanced up sharply. "You mean we're not just running—we're *going back* in?"

Matthias nodded. "The safe house in Mainz is near the old brewery. From there, we can plan the interception. If we succeed, it could save hundreds."

Anna looked from one man to the next. "And if we fail?"

Matthias's expression didn't waver. "Then at least we'll fall trying to make it matter."

Thunder rolled again, closer now.

Anna turned back to Lukas, who was watching her quietly, rain glinting in his lashes. "You heard him," he said softly. "We're not done yet."

She wanted to argue, to tell him he needed rest, that his leg would never hold—but the fire in his eyes stopped her.

"All right," she said. "We reach Mainz. Then we fight."

Matthias rose, tucking the paper back inside his coat. "We move before the patrols cross the bridge. Keep low and follow my light."

They left the shelter as the wind howled through the fields. The world was nothing but rain, thunder, and the rhythm of footsteps—tired, defiant, unbroken.

Ahead lay Mainz, the city of smoke and stone—and whatever waited in its shadow.

CHAPTER TWENTY-FIVE:
Arrival in Mainz

The storm had dulled to a cold drizzle by the time they reached the outskirts of Mainz. Smoke clung low to the chimneys, and the streets were slick with rain and mud.

Matthias led them through the narrow alleys, avoiding the main square where German soldiers gathered around carts and barrels of coal. The city smelled of ash and bread, exhaustion and fear.

"Almost there," he whispered. "Stay close. No sudden movements."

They slipped through a row of shuttered houses to the old brewery district. The sign over the door—Hahn & Söhne Brauerei—was faded, the windows boarded, but a faint glow leaked from the cracks below the door.

Matthias knocked twice, paused, then twice again.

A narrow panel slid open. "Password?"

"Eisenherz," he murmured.

The bolt slid back. They entered quickly, one by one.

Inside, the air was damp and warm. Candles burned in the cellar, lighting a scattering of weary faces—men and women in worn coats, huddled around a table covered in maps and ration tins.

"Matthias," the man at the head of the table said, standing to greet him. "You made it."

"Barely," Matthias replied. "We brought survivors. The Müller family—Anna's parents—and one wounded soldier."

The man's eyes softened. "You're safe here," he said to Anna. "At least for a night. We have food and dry blankets. Rest while you can."

Anna helped Lukas lower himself onto a bench near the stove. Her mother knelt beside him, checking his bandage with the practiced hands of a nurse.

"You'll live," she murmured, a faint smile breaking through her exhaustion. "If you rest."

"For now," Lukas said weakly, and she smiled again.

Erich leaned his rifle against the wall. "What's the situation here?"

The man—Johann Reuter, the local resistance contact—lowered his voice. "We've been watching the rail lines. There's movement—something big. Command wants us to stay quiet until we know more."

Matthias frowned. "More troops?"

"No. A transfer. A prisoner convoy is heading east tomorrow night. We don't know who or why, but Berlin requested it directly."

Anna glanced up, uneasy. "Then we're not staying long."

Johann nodded. "You'll move again before dawn tomorrow, once the next route is clear. The others will stay here until we can arrange passage." He looked at Anna's parents.

"You'll be safe below ground. The patrols rarely search the brewery."

Her mother exhaled in relief. "Gott sei Dank."

Anna placed a hand on her father's arm. "You'll rest here. I'll help Matthias prepare for the next leg."

Her father's brow furrowed. "You mean to keep moving?"

She nodded. "There's still work to do."

Lukas caught her hand, his voice low. "Not without me."

She smiled faintly. "We'll see what Johann says in the morning."

Thunder rolled again in the distance—faint, like a memory. The group settled into uneasy quiet, the storm dripping from the cellar stairs and the smell of yeast lingering in the air.

For the first time in days, Anna's parents could rest. Lukas, too, drifted toward sleep beside the stove. But Matthias and Johann stayed bent over the maps, their voices low and grim.

And when Anna caught the words *prisoner transfer through Mainz*—something in her heart stirred. Whatever peace they had found here would not last.

* * *

Matthias spread the damp map across the table. "We can't stay here long," he said. "They'll be combing the outskirts by morning."

Erich frowned. "We just escaped a city crawling with patrols. Where do you suggest we go?"

Matthias tapped the map. "There's a supply route heading west—toward Bingen. The resistance has another network there. If we can make it across the river, we can regroup and send word to Command."

Anna's father leaned forward. "That means crossing open ground. No bridges, not with the army tightening control."

"Then we move by night," Matthias said. "There's an old railway tunnel near Ober-Ingelheim—half collapsed, but passable. It'll get us under the line."

Anna's mother looked from him to Anna. "And then? What happens when we reach the next safe house?"

Matthias hesitated. "That depends. There's talk of a prisoner transport—something moving east out of Mainz tomorrow night. If the rumors are true, Command will want us close."

Anna's father exchanged a worried look with her. "Back to Mainz?"

Matthias nodded grimly. "Only if we have no choice."

The room fell quiet again. Outside, the wind howled through the cracks, rattling the shutters.

Anna sank beside Lukas on the bench. He took her hand, his thumb tracing slow circles across her knuckles.

"We just got out," she whispered. "And already they're talking about going back."

His voice was low, rough. "That's what war does. You leave one fire only to run toward another."

She rested her head against his shoulder.

Matthias rolled up the map and doused the lamp. "Rest while you can," he said quietly. "Tomorrow, the road begins again."

* * *

The storm had eased to a steady drizzle, but the air inside the cellar still smelled of rain and gun oil. Matthias fastened the straps on his pack with the precision of a man who didn't want to think. Erich checked the ammunition belt twice, muttering to himself.

Anna laid out the bandages Lukas would need through the night. Her hands moved quickly, but he could see the tremor in them.

"You're leaving me here," Lukas said, his voice low and raw.

Matthias didn't look up. "You can't move faster than a crawl, and the wound will slow us all down. We can't afford that tonight."

"I can cover you from a distance—"

"From the floor?" Matthias's tone was sharp, but there was no malice in it, only fear disguised as anger. "You'll stay here. With the Müllers and the others. Keep the lamps dark. If we're not back by dawn, you take whoever's left and disappear."

Lukas clenched his jaw, staring at the maps spread across the table. "You think I'll sit here while you risk your lives for a ghost?"

Erich slung his rifle over his shoulder. "Not a ghost. A man, Command says, could turn the tide. We don't know his name, only his file number—' T-47. 'They say he was high in the Ministry before he vanished. That's all we've got."

Anna knelt beside Lukas, her hand light on his arm. "Please," she said softly. "You'll help us more by being alive when we get back."

For a moment, neither of them moved. The lantern flame shivered between them, painting the walls in gold and shadow.

Finally, Lukas nodded once, a stiff, reluctant gesture. "Fine. But if you're not back by dawn, I'm coming for you."

Matthias met his eyes. "Fair enough."

They moved toward the stairs, their boots whispering against the floor. Anna turned at the door, her face pale in the lantern light. "Lock the back door after us," she said. "And no heroics, Lukas."

He tried to smile. "Too late for that."

When the door shut and the sound of their steps faded, the safe house fell silent except for the ticking of rain. Lukas sat in the half-dark, his hands pressed to his bandaged thigh, listening to the storm and the ghosts of gunfire it carried.

He had never felt more useless — or more afraid.

* * *

Rain fell in needles, whispering against the corrugated roofs of the Mainz rail yard. The air reeked of coal smoke and wet iron. Freight cars loomed like sleeping beasts, their silhouettes blurred by mist.

Matthias led the way, a dark shape under a stolen overcoat, Erich close behind with a satchel of charges wrapped in oilcloth. Anna moved with them, the hem of her nurse's coat soaked and heavy, her breath frosting the air. They had memorized every step: across the yard, under the siding, to the storage shed where the Gestapo held prisoners for transfer.

The world narrowed to small sounds — the click of Erich's lighter, the whisper of boots on gravel, the distant cough of a guard's cigarette.

"Two on the north gate," Matthias murmured. "We wait for the shift change."

Anna pressed her back to the wall. Inside, through a slit in the boards, she saw the convoy truck idling — three guards, one driver, and a man hunched between them in chains. The headlights cut pale slices through the rain.

"That's him?" Erich whispered.

Matthias nodded. "T-47. Move."

They crossed the yard like shadows. The thunder rolled, perfectly timed to hide the crack of Matthias's suppressed pistol. One guard dropped; another turned and fell into Erich's arms before he could shout. The third stumbled backward, clutching his rifle. Anna stepped out from the dark, steady and calm, the syringe already in her hand. The needle found his neck before he could raise the alarm.

For a moment, there was silence again — only the patter of rain on the truck's hood.

Matthias yanked the rear door open. "Get him out."

The prisoner blinked up at them, gaunt, his face obscured by mud and bruises. A transport tag hung from his collar, the letters smeared: T-47. Anna reached to steady him as Matthias cut the chain at his wrists.

"You're safe," she said, though she wasn't sure it was true.

He looked at her through a curtain of wet hair. "Safe?" His voice was a rasp. "No one's safe now. You don't know what they're moving."

Erich frowned. "We're here for you, not riddles. Can you walk?"

The prisoner nodded, swaying. "I'll manage. But if you've come for me, you'll have company soon."

Headlights flared at the far end of the yard — another truck turning in. Matthias cursed under his breath. "They changed the schedule."

"Back way!" Anna shouted. She and Erich half-dragged, half-carried the prisoner through the maze of freight cars while gunfire cracked across the yard. Sparks danced from the rails. Matthias fired once, twice, covering them as they ducked into the drainage tunnel.

They ran until their breath came in gasps, until the thunder swallowed the sound of pursuit. The tunnel spilled them into the riverbank north of the city, the water biting cold around their boots.

Matthias turned to make sure everyone was there: Anna, pale but unhurt; Erich, bleeding from a graze on his arm; and the prisoner, staring back toward Mainz with haunted eyes.

"Who are you?" Matthias demanded.

The man drew a shaking breath. "My name doesn't matter. What they're building does." He looked down at the mud, voice barely a whisper. "Get me to your Command. And pray we're not too late."

* * *

The wagon groaned over the rutted track, its wheels splashing through puddles that mirrored the gray of dawn. The storm had passed, leaving the air thick and cold. Steam rose from the horses 'flanks.

Matthias sat at the reins, eyes on the narrow road twisting through the forest. Erich dozed upright in the back, his wounded arm bound tight, the rifle still clutched across his knees. Anna pressed a damp cloth to the prisoner's forehead, watching him with a nurse's instinct and a spy's suspicion.

"Keep that pace," Matthias called over his shoulder. "The patrols will be sweeping the city by now."

T-47's eyes opened. They were a startling, icy blue — clear even under the grime. "They'll find the bodies at the yard," he said quietly. "That will buy you an hour. Maybe two."

Anna frowned. "You seem sure of their timing."

He gave a faint, humorless smile. "I should be. I helped write their schedules."

Matthias turned. "You were Gestapo?"

"Not by choice. Ministry of Intelligence, Berlin section. My real name—" He stopped, as if the words weighed more than breath. "Call me Theo. They used my research to hunt the Resistance. I tried to destroy it when I fled. That's why they want me alive."

Erich blinked away sleep. "Research? What kind of research?"

Theo's fingers tightened around the blanket Anna had wrapped him in. "They're building something. A system of codes tied to transport schedules, supply depots, and deportation routes. Once complete, it will make every arrest, every shipment invisible — no paper trail, no witness left alive."

Matthias's face hardened. "And you can stop it?"

"I can expose it," Theo said. "If I reach your Command. But you need to understand: they'll send everything after me now. You should have left me in that yard."

Anna met his gaze. "We don't leave people behind."

Theo studied her, a flicker of something — respect, perhaps guilt — passing across his expression. "Then pray your wounded friend keeps quiet. If he's captured, they'll tear this network apart name by name."

Matthias said nothing. The only sound was the creak of the wheels and the low murmur of the river beyond the trees. Above them, the first light of morning spread thin and colorless across the sky.

"Two hours," Theo said again. "After that, your safe house won't be safe."

CHAPTER TWENTY-SIX
Captured

They stumbled in from the rain just before dawn, boots slapping mud onto the stone floor. The air was thick with smoke from the spent lanterns and the metallic scent of blood that clung to them after the night's fighting. Anna's hands shook as she shoved the cellar door shut behind Erich. For the first time in hours, she allowed herself to breathe.

Matthias dropped his pack and leaned against the wall, eyes hollow. "We made it," he said, as if saying it might make it true.

Anna moved first—past the table, toward the small cot where Lukas should have been. The blanket lay half-tossed aside, still holding the shape of his body. The basin of water she'd left for him had gone cold.

"Lukas?" Her voice cracked. She crossed the room, checked the dark corner where her parents had been resting. Empty. The coat her father wore was gone. Her mother's shawl still hung from the peg, damp with the night air seeping in.

"Stay here," Matthias said to Erich and Anna. "If anything's wrong, we don't linger."

He eased the cellar door open. The hinges groaned. The smell of damp earth and burnt oil met him, the same smell they had lived with for weeks. But something else too—stillness. No voices. No Lukas.

"Lukas?" Anna called softly from behind him as she slipped through the doorway. Her boots left muddy prints on the stone floor. The lantern was still burning on the table, the flame small and steady. The cot in the corner lay unmade, the blanket half on the floor.

"Where are they?" Erich's voice cracked. He crossed the room quickly, checking the stairs, the kitchen, the small side chamber where her parents had slept. "Nothing. They're gone."

Anna's breath caught. Her mother's shawl still hung by the door. The tea kettle sat cold on the stove, half full. "They wouldn't have left that."

Matthias crouched near the back door, fingertips brushing the splintered wood. "Latch is broken," he murmured. "Forced from the outside."

Theo stood in the doorway, his face unreadable. "You said this place was safe."

"It was," Erich snapped. "Only three people knew—"

"Then one of them talked," Theo said flatly.

The words hung in the air like smoke.

Anna turned slowly, her eyes wide and bright in the lamplight. "Lukas would never—"

Matthias raised a hand. "No one's accusing anyone. But they're gone, and the Gestapo won't stop until they've turned this whole quarter inside out."

Anna moved to the cot, touching the empty blanket. It was still warm. "They didn't take his coat," she whispered. "He wouldn't have left it."

Theo stepped closer, studying the tracks on the floor — boot prints smeared with mud, one dragging as if someone had been limping. "Whoever came for them moved fast."

Matthias straightened, jaw set. "Then we move faster. If Lukas and her parents are alive, they'll be taken to Command headquarters. That's where we start."

Anna looked at the broken door again, at the space where Lukas should have been. Her voice trembled, but her words were hard. "Then we finish what we started in Mainz. We go back."

Outside, thunder rolled distantly over the river. The sun broke through the clouds, pale and cold. Inside the safe house, the flickering lantern burned low, its light trembling on the empty cot.

The back door hung slightly ajar, the wood splintered where the latch should have held. A single hinge squealed in the draft. Muddy footprints led out into the alley—two large, one lighter, dragging.

Anna's stomach twisted. She knelt, touching the broken latch with trembling fingers. "Lukas," she whispered. "My parents,"

Erich's hand went to his pistol. "Could be they ran— maybe Lukas heard something and tried to get your parents out."

"Or he couldn't walk," Matthias said grimly. "They could've taken all three."

The lantern flame caught the edge of his knife as he closed it. The sound was soft, final. "Pack what you can carry. We can't stay."

Anna rose slowly, her face pale but her eyes hardening. "And Johann? We're not running again," she said. "We find them."

Rain hammered against the door, the world outside already lightening toward a gray morning. The three of them stood in the flickering glow—exhausted, filthy, half-frozen—but alive. Behind them, the cellar lay empty, the blanket still warm where Lukas had been.

* * *

By evening, the storm had rolled east, leaving only the wind. The safe house had gone silent again except for the rhythmic ticking of the clock above the cold stove. They gathered around the table where maps and ration scraps lay scattered, the paper still damp from the rain.

Matthias leaned over the spread of charts, a cigarette burning low between his fingers. "They won't keep them here in Mainz," he said. "If the Gestapo took Lukas, he's on his way to Berlin—or worse, to Prinz-Albrecht-Strasse."

Erich swore softly. "That's the center of their whole command. We'd be walking straight into hell."

"That's where they'll take the important prisoners." Matthias tapped the map. "If Lukas or the Müllers are alive, that's where they'll be interrogated—and where Theo's information will matter most."

Theo sat in the corner, coat wrapped around him, eyes hollow. "You're talking about the central headquarters of the RSHA. Layers of security, coded passes, checkpoints every fifty meters. You can't storm it."

Matthias met his gaze. "No. We slip in. The way you did when you worked for them."

Theo hesitated, then gave a bitter laugh. "You have no idea what you're asking."

"I'm asking for a way in," Matthias said. "You said they'll destroy every trace of that code system if they suspect you've survived. That means the files are still there—and so are our people."

Erich shook his head. "We don't have the men, the guns—"

"Then we use what we have," Matthias cut in. "Uniforms, forged papers, Theo's credentials. A small team— Anna, you, me, Theo. We'll pose as a medical transport moving prisoners for re-evaluation. Once we're inside, we find Lukas, Johann, and the Müllers, get them out, and burn the records room on the way."

The silence that followed felt heavy enough to crush the air. Anna stared at him, pale but steady. "And if it's a trap?"

"Then we go down fighting for something that still matters," Matthias said quietly. "They took everything from us once already. I won't let them do it again."

Theo looked between them, his expression unreadable. "If we go to Berlin, you'll need more than courage. You'll need to think like them. I can get you through the first door—but after that, you're on your own."

Matthias stubbed out his cigarette. "Then we start tonight. We've got one shot before they move Lukas deeper into the system."

Anna's voice was barely above a whisper. "We're really going to Berlin."

Matthias looked at her—tired, haunted, unbreakable. "Into the heart of it," he said. "And we don't come back without them."

:

CHAPTER TWENTY-SEVEN:
Gestapo Headquarters
Interrogation

The bulb above him buzzed like an angry wasp. Lukas kept his eyes on it because it was the only steady thing in the room. His hands were tied to the chair. The rope had already rubbed the skin raw.

The door opened. The same officer stepped in, coat unbuttoned now, his voice almost casual. "You had a quiet hour to think, Schneider. Did it help you remember where your friends hide?"

Lukas shook his head. "You already know what I know."

The officer sighs and nodded to the two soldiers behind him. They moved closer, boots echoing on the concrete. One tilts Lukas's chin up with the tip of a truncheon.
"Still proud," he says. "Let us see how long pride breathes."

The first blow drove the air from Lukas's lungs; the second landed against his ribs, where the bone never set right. The third caught his thigh. Pain flashed white, his vision blurred, and the reopened wound spilled warmth down his leg. He tasted copper and grit, and heard the slow creak of his own breath.

"Names," the officer says.

Lukas's answer was a whisper. "No."

Another strike. The rope cut deeper. The world narrowed to the throb in his leg, the drip of water, the smell of dust and iron.

They unwrapped the dressing on his thigh without ceremony, ripping the gauze away sticky and dark; the wound beneath was a raw line against his thigh, swollen and angry in the lamplight. Air touched it, and his breath caught — not from drama, but the simple, exacting recognition of exposed tissue.

The officer set the small brown bottle on the table and removed the cap with a practised motion. The scent unfurled immediately: sharp, chemical, clinical. He tilted the bottle, and the liquid fell in a steady thread. Where it met flesh, there was no cinematic splash, only a precise, searing contraction — a reflexive expulsion of sound that surprised Lukas by how small it was. His hands tightened on the edge of the chair; his fingers whitened.

They did not shout. No one raised their voice. The guard's glove pressed once, twice, to check for reaction. The officer watched, cool and methodical, as if reading vitals. Lukas felt the burn move through him like heat running under cloth: hot, quick, then alive with a brittle, electrical edge that left his muscles trembling. He tasted iron at the back of his mouth, breathed short and even, counting to himself in a slow cadence he'd learned in the field to steady panicked limbs.

Between the rinses of iodine and the brief, efficient questioning, they doused him with cold water to clear the fog of pain. Each cold wash reset the margin of endurance; each re-exposure to the antiseptic redefined it. They alternated these clinical measures with blunt strikes — not to gore, but to disorient — and in the pauses Lukas folded inward, putting his attention on the only things he could control: the rhythm of his breathing, the remembered shape of Anna's hand on his thigh, the stubborn, silent answer he would not give.

When they finally rebandaged him, it was with the same unemotional care as when they'd removed the dressing. The iodine's smell lingered in the room and in his clothes; his skin prickled where it had touched him. He sat very still, pulse loud in his ears, and let the pain be a fact he acknowledged rather than a thing that could command him.

"Your friend is not so stubborn," the officer lied. "He told us everything. You bleed for nothing."

Lukas forced a laugh that sounded more like a gasp. "Then why… still ask?"

For a moment, the officer's face hardened. He gestures for the guards to stop, wipes his gloves clean with a handkerchief. "Very well. Keep your silence. We'll question him again in the morning. Perhaps he'll enjoy hearing what you've endured for him."

He turned to leave. The soldiers threw a bucket of cold water over Lukas, washing blood and sweat into a puddle. He slumped forward, the ropes the only thing keeping him upright.

When the door finally clanked shut, the silence rushed back. Lukas dragged in a breath, every muscle shaking. The pain hummed through him, dull and constant, but somewhere beneath it is a flicker of grim satisfaction: *They still don't know.*

He stared at the faint strip of light under the door, thinking of Johann and the Müllers down the corridor, and of Anna—her promise, her fire.
He murmured through cracked lips, "You'll find me. You always do."

* * *

The road unfurled gray and endless beneath a low, colorless sky. The landscape had flattened to fields and scattered woods, washed pale by the winter light. A cold wind pressed against the truck's canvas sides, carrying the scent of diesel and rain.

No one spoke for a long time. The motor's steady grind filled the silence. Anna sat in the back beside a crate of medical supplies, her gloved hands folded in her lap. Across from her, Theo watched the fields roll by through the slit in the tarp, face drawn and unreadable.

Matthias drove, his shoulders rigid, eyes on the ribbon of road ahead. Erich sat beside him, radio parts and forged papers piled at his feet. Every few kilometers, they passed a checkpoint or a convoy heading the other way—columns of soldiers, supply wagons, officers in long coats that gleamed like oil. Each time, Matthias's hands tightened on the wheel, and Anna felt her pulse match the rhythm of the tires against the road.

Theo finally broke the silence. "Once we cross into the city, you follow my lead. Speak only when spoken to. The uniforms and permits will get you through the first gates, nothing more."

Matthias gave a small nod without looking away from the road. "After that?"

Theo hesitated. "After that, it depends on who recognizes me."

Anna met his eyes. "You think they still will?"

A faint smile touched his mouth, brittle and humorless. "I designed half their clearance systems. They'll remember my face."

Erich exhaled sharply. "That's supposed to make us feel better?"

"No," Theo said. "It's supposed to make you careful."

The wind shifted, rattling the truck's canvas. Anna pulled her coat tighter. She could feel the ache in her shoulders, the exhaustion creeping in after days without real rest, but beneath it all was something sharper—fear and the thin, bright thread of determination. Lukas. Her parents. Somewhere inside the vast machinery of Berlin's authority, they were alive or they weren't. And she would find out which.

Matthias spoke at last, his voice quiet but certain. "Once we reach the city, there's no turning back. Whatever happens after this—we finish it."

Anna nodded, her gaze fixed on the horizon where the first gray spires of the capital were beginning to rise out of the haze. The sky above them was a hard, metallic blue.

"Then we finish it," she said.

The truck rumbled on, small against the breadth of the empty road, carrying four people toward the heart of everything they feared.

* * *

They had stripped him to his undershirt. His wounded side was wrapped in filthy bandages that had once been white. Sweat darkened his hair, and one of his eyes had already begun to swell shut. He stood between two soldiers, wrists bound above him to a hook in the ceiling.

The officer approached. "Herr Schneider," he said, in that same cool tone. "You were seen near the rail yard explosion in Mainz. You were found with forged orders and an English medallion. You will tell us what unit you serve with, and who sent you."

248

Lukas spat blood onto the floor. "I serve Germany. Not you."

The first blow came from the side — a baton to the ribs. He gasped, his legs nearly buckling. They hit him again, methodically, letting the silence stretch between each strike so that the sound of his breathing became the only noise in the room.

"You think your silence is noble?" the officer asked. "Your friends will break. They always do. You are only hastening their pain."

Lukas lifted his head, blood running down his chin. "Then you don't know them."

That earned him another hit — harder this time, across the stomach. He doubled forward, choking, but didn't beg. Somewhere in his mind, through the haze, he saw Anna — the field light on her face, the warmth of her hand when she bandaged him the first time. *Hold on,* he told himself *for her.*

When they finally unhooked him, he fell to his knees, unable to catch himself. The officer crouched down beside him. "You could make this end. Just one name."

Lukas coughed, laughed faintly, the sound raw. "You first."

The officer straightened, disgusted. "Again tomorrow," he said to the guards. "If he's still conscious."

As they dragged him away, he caught a glimpse of Johann through the open doorway across the corridor — his head bowed, his hands trembling, but his eyes meeting his. It was enough. He nodded once before they pulled him out of sight.

* * *

The room smelled faintly of antiseptic and cold metal. Abraham Müller sat at the small desk where they'd left him, his spectacles bent from handling, a stack of typed reports before him. The papers bore headings in sharp black ink—statistics, quotas, clinical terminology designed to bury horror under precision.

He had been told to review them, to make notes, to give "scientific perspective." What they meant was *approval*. He refused. The notes he wrote were useless on purpose— measurements that contradicted themselves, margins filled with obscure Latin, a slow, silent rebellion typed in neat lines no one read closely.

A guard's boots passed in the corridor outside. The sound echoed off the tiled walls. Abraham set the pen down, rubbing the bridge of his nose, and listened. Two doors away, someone coughed—a dry, familiar sound. Miriam.

They allowed him to see her once a day, for ten minutes, in the small examination room between the wards. Always a guard in the corner, a table between them. They weren't allowed to speak in anything but German, in simple phrases, nothing political. Still, he found ways. Her hands trembled when she poured tea, but her eyes told him what he needed to know: she was alive, she was enduring, she believed Anna had escaped.

That afternoon, the guard escorted him down the corridor to her cell. She was sitting by the narrow window, the weak winter light outlining her hair. When she saw him, she stood quickly, smoothing her dress as if she could make the place respectable by force of will.

"Abraham," she said softly.

He took her hands through the bars. "They haven't hurt you?"

"Not yet. They think I'm harmless." A faint smile, weary and brave. "How are your papers coming?"

"As useless as possible."

Her smile flickered. "Good."

They fell quiet for a moment. Beyond the courtyard wall, a train whistle sounded—long, distant, final. Miriam closed her eyes. "Do you think she's still free?"

"I have to believe she is," he said. "If I stop believing, they've already won."

A key turned in the lock behind him. The guard cleared his throat. "Time."

Abraham squeezed her fingers once more before letting go. "Hold on," he whispered. "Whatever happens—hold on."

The door closed, and the corridor swallowed her face again. He walked back to his room without looking at the guards, the notes in his pocket a secret language of resistance.

* * *

They came for him before dawn, when the cell was at its coldest and the world outside still belonged to rain and shadow. A guard hauled him upright, and the ropes bit into his wrists as they were slung over a hook; the weight pinned his shoulders and turned every breath into labor. The light above the table buzzed like a trapped insect. The same officer stood there, hands folded, voice low and patient as a judge reading names.

251

"Schneider," he said. "We have been patient."

Lukas tasted metal on his tongue and felt the old bandages give when they tore them away. Air hit the wound, and something bright and white flared across his nerves. A guard pressed a gloved finger where the flesh had already been raw; the pressure made him see stars. When the bottle came, it was small and brown and ordinary. The officer uncapped it, and the iodine's acrid sting poured into the open seam of his thigh. The sound it made—no splash, more like a hiss—was worse than the pain that followed. Lukas could not stop the sound that left him, a single animal cry that the room swallowed without sympathy.

They beat him in measured intervals, not to kill but to hollow out his resistance: blunt strikes across ribs and gut, timed so his lungs filled with air and then were knocked loose again, each pause a question answered with silence. Between blows, they doused him with cold water until the shiver settled into his bones and sleep became impossible.

Once, a boot drove a spike of pressure into the wound itself; the guard twisted and pressed as if searching for some hidden thing. Lukas hands fisted with fingers gone numb, his mind sliding into the one place that kept pain at bay — Anna's face in lamplight, her hands moving steady and clean, the faint joke she'd made about his stubbornness. *Hold on*, he told himself, over and over, the mantra of breath and muscle.

They used his comrades as shadows in their speech. "We could return them to you," the officer murmured, nodding toward the next cell as if they were a trinket on the table. "See them—alive—if you help." They slid documents and lists across the table, names, addresses, some crossed out; a photograph, a smear of someone else's blood on a scrap of gauze. They told stories of transfers, of camps, of "mistakes" that became permanent. Each suggestion was a tool: the promise of mercy dangled, the threat of worse made casual.

When he tried to answer with bluff and fury, they shifted—soft voices, precise questions, then the sudden weight of a baton. They kept him off balance by alternating cruelty and seeming reason; the officer's calm sentences about logistics felt more dangerous than the guards 'shouts. Once, the officer stood face to face and said, almost kindly, "If you name them, it ends. Think of the nurse. Think of your old woman." The words landed like blows aimed not at flesh but at the small, private things he could not bear to imagine broken.

Between cycles of brutality, they left him to hang until the ropes dug deeper, until the skin at his wrists burned. Fever came, low and insistent: the wound throbbed, swelling, a hot, angry bloom beneath the skin in the filthy light of the room. Every removal of a dressing was an announcement of exposure; every reapplication was a reminder that they controlled his healing. Sleep drifted in thin, dangerous edges—until they woke him again with a bucket, the cold washing away the blankness and replacing it with a fresh, clean panic.

They tried to make him bargaining currency: "Names for life," they said. "Names for the sight of Anna." And when their threats were not enough, they used the others— or the rumor of them being in the next room — as an instrument of dread. He heard, once, the muffled ragged breath of someone close by and imagined it was them, and the image of them bent and trembling unmoored him for a second; then he latched onto something else.

When the session finally eased, they left him slumped, wrists chafed, jaw aching, each breath a small victory. The officer stood a moment in the doorway and said with a quiet certainty, "Tomorrow will be clearer." Lukas answered only once, his voice a crack in the air: "Is the name you want Mickey Mouse?"

It was not bravado so much as a promise— he would not give them away. He closed his eyes and clung to memory until the pain thinned into something he could carry. When the guards dragged him back toward the cell, the iodine smell followed him like a brand. But even as his legs failed and his breath shortened, the defiance in his chest did not.

Time lost its shape inside those walls.
Days—or maybe only nights—blurred together in the same dim light, the same measured cruelty. They never let the wounds close: each morning, a new dressing torn away, a fresh sting of antiseptic poured into flesh already burning. When the questions came, they were the same, but the silences between them grew longer, heavier.

Sleep was a rumor. Food came as scraps he could barely swallow. The cold seeped into his bones, while fever made the air shimmer like heat over a battlefield. He counted breaths instead of hours, the sound of boots instead of the ticking of a clock. Once or twice, he thought he heard Anna's voice down the hall—soft, pleading—but the guards only laughed when he called her name.

By the fifth day, his body was a collection of tremors and bruises, his mind a single, stubborn thread. They wanted names; he gave them none. They wanted surrender; he offered silence. When they left him hanging between waking and sleep, he whispered to the darkness the only thing that still mattered: *Hold on. She's coming.*

CHAPTER TWENTY-EIGHT
Berlin

The city appeared first as a smear of smoke and chimneys, its air thick with coal and fear. By the time they reached the outskirts, the daylight had dimmed to a metallic dusk. Checkpoints came every few kilometers; uniforms, dogs, questions. Each time Theo handled the papers with practiced calm, and each time the guards waved them through.

Inside the cab, the silence grew heavy. When they stopped at a derelict fuel depot to rest, Theo pulled a folded sheet from his coat — a requisition form he'd lifted from the checkpoint officer's clipboard. His eyes scanned it quickly, lips moving.

"Transfer schedules," he murmured. "Two prisoners from Mainz. Designated for medical evaluation under Keller's authority."

He looked up, the color draining from his face. "The names are Abraham and Miriam Müller."

Anna's breath caught; the world seemed to tilt. "My parents."

Theo folded the paper, his voice quiet but urgent. "They're at the same annex where Lukas will be. The one Keller runs. If we go in, we have one chance—one corridor, one extraction. After that, the whole complex will be sealed."

Matthias met Anna's eyes. "Then we go. All of them or none."

Erich checked his pistol, jaw tight. "I'd say we've come too far to stop."

The rain began again, soft at first, then harder against the truck's roof. Theo looked toward the darkening skyline where the government buildings rose like stone sentinels. "Once we cross that bridge," he said, "there's no way back."

Anna answered without hesitation. "There never was."

They entered at dawn under forged orders and borrowed coats. The corridors smelled of disinfectant and electricity. Theo walked in front, his pace measured, his badge visible. Guards nodded without suspicion; the paperwork was perfect.

In the lower wing, he paused outside a locked door. "Here," he said. "Records room. Lukas and the Müllers are listed on this floor."

Matthias and Erich moved to cover the corridor. Anna followed Theo into the room. The ledgers were stacked neatly, the ink precise and cold. She found the entry: *Schneider, Lukas — interrogation scheduled, transfer pending.* Below it, *Müller, Abraham, and Miriam— medical annex, section C.*

"They're alive," she whispered.

Theo's hand closed over hers, briefly. "Then let's not waste it."

They moved fast. The guards in the cell block never expected resistance to come from wearing the right uniforms. Matthias struck first, swift and silent. Anna reached Lukas's cell, the key cold in her fingers. When the door opened, he looked up from the cot, thinner, paler, but still him. For a heartbeat, neither spoke; then she crossed the distance and caught his face in her hands.

"You came," he breathed.

"Of course I did."

Matthias and Erich each pulled Lucas between them. They freed Anna's parents next — Miriam, weak but walking, Abraham carrying the same battered case of false reports. Alarm bells began to ring somewhere above them. Theo turned toward the stairs. "They've found the forged credentials. We have minutes."

"Then we move!" Matthias said.

They ran through the corridors, gunfire echoing behind them, the smell of cordite mixing with the sting of iodine and smoke. Outside, dawn bled pale over the city. Erich climbed into the truck, firing the engine alive. Theo lingered at the door, tearing a bundle of coded files from the wall and setting them alight.

"For the record," he said quietly. "Let it burn."

They drove until Berlin disappeared behind them, swallowed by fog and distance. Only when the last checkpoint faded in the mirrors did anyone speak.

Miriam leaned against Abraham's shoulder. Lukas reached for Anna's hand. Theo watched the smoke rising from the city they'd left behind and said, almost to himself, "Now they'll have to write a new story."

Spring, 1945

The bells rang first, a thin, uncertain sound from the village church, echoing through the valley. By noon, the rumor had become fact: the war was over. German units were laying down their arms, and the last columns had withdrawn beyond the river. The guns were silent.

At the farmhouse on the hill, the air smelled of earth and rain, of bread baking and the faintest trace of lilac from the hedgerows. Inside, Anna stood at the kitchen table, sleeves rolled, carving roasted goose while steam clouded the windowpanes. Her mother basted the meat one last time, humming a tune that had survived the blackout years in whispers. The old clock ticked steadily above them, unbothered by history.

The door opened and sunlight spilled across the floorboards. Lukas stood there, his limp still pronounced but his face clearer, younger somehow. He smelled of the road and spring mud, and when Anna turned, he grinned the way he once had before the war had hollowed everyone's laughter.

His parents and brother were with him, and he introduced them around.

"Erich found wine," he announced. "Actual wine, not vinegar with a label."

From outside came Matthias's rough voice: "You make one joke and you pour your own glass, Captain." He entered, carrying a crate in each arm, followed by Erich with his usual crooked smile and Lisete.

The table filled quickly—bread, roasted potatoes, the goose glistening under its crisp skin, apples baked in the pan beside it. Theo had gone north weeks before, but his name was raised in a silent toast. When Abraham poured the wine, his hands no longer trembled. Miriam placed a dish of cabbage before him, brushed his sleeve, and said softly, "Sit. For once, sit."

They ate slowly at first, as though uncertain the moment was real. Outside, the fields lay in a soft haze of green; birds had returned to the orchard. The silence between words felt new, not hollow but peaceful. It was Matthias who broke it, lifting his glass.

"To the living," he said. "And to the ones who brought us home."

Erich clinked his cup against Lisete's. "And to no more trains," he added quietly. They drank to that.

Later, as dusk settled and the candles burned low, Lukas leaned back in his chair, the firelight turning his scars to faint shadows. "I used to think the only things a man could carry from war were ghosts," he said. "But maybe it's this instead— bread, wine, the sound of people laughing again."

Anna smiled. "And maybe a reminder of what's worth saving."

He reached across the table, found her hand. Outside, the church bell rang again, steady now, its sound drifting through the open window. Around them, the room smelled of roast goose and rain-damp wood, of home rebuilt from ruin.

For the first time in years, they didn't speak of what had been lost.

They simply ate, and listened to the quiet, and let the peace take hold.

Epilogue:
Spring, 1946

The farmhouse outside Wiesbaden was quiet, surrounded by the first green of the season. The war had ended months ago, but the land was still healing. Anna stood at the open window, the air cool and clean. Behind her, Lukas slept in the chair by the stove, the scar on his thigh pale against the firelight.

Matthias and Erich were already on the road again — rebuilding what was left of the Resistance into something new. Theo had gone north to testify, to name the men who had built the system he'd helped to destroy. The Müllers tended a small clinic nearby, treating whoever came through the valley, no questions asked.

Anna turned back toward Lukas and smiled faintly. "You should be in bed," she said.

He stirred, eyes opening. "I wanted to hear the rain."

Outside, the first drops began — soft and gentle. She crossed to him, took his hand, and the two of them sat in silence while the world, at last, began to mend.

In the years that followed, the medals tarnished and the uniforms disappeared into trunks, but what endured could not be polished or pinned. Lukas carried the memory of the iron cross he had once worn — a token from a war that tried to claim his soul — and beside it, the simple locket Anna had given him, warm from her hand and shaped like a heart. One was a relic of duty; the other, of love. Between them lay everything they had lost and everything they had saved.

And when the world finally learned to breathe again, those who knew their story said they were the proof that even in an age of iron, a heart of gold could still prevail.

www.ingramcontent.com/pod-product-compliance
Lightning Source LLC
Chambersburg PA
CBHW072349020726
47506CB00004B/1066